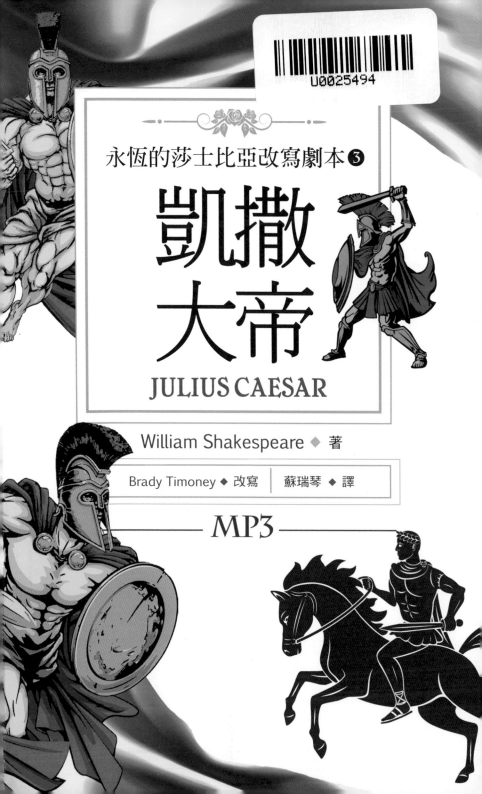

永恆的莎士比亞改寫劇本 ❸

凱撒大帝

JULIUS CAESAR

William Shakespeare ◆ 著

Brady Timoney ◆ 改寫　｜　蘇瑞琴 ◆ 譯

MP3

永恆的莎士比亞改寫劇本 ❸
凱撒大帝
JULIUS CAESAR

作　　者	William Shakespeare, Brady Timoney
翻　　譯	蘇瑞琴
編　　輯	Gina Wang
校　　對	丁宥榆
內文排版	林書玉
封面設計	林書玉
製程管理	洪巧玲
出 版 者	寂天文化事業股份有限公司
電　　話	+886-(0)2-2365-9739
傳　　真	+886-(0)2-2365-9835
網　　址	www.icosmos.com.tw
讀者服務	onlineservice@icosmos.com.tw
出版日期	2016 年 8 月 初版一刷

郵撥帳號 1998620-0 寂天文化事業股份有限公司
劃撥金額 600（含）元以上者，郵資免費。
訂購金額 600 元以下者，加收 65 元運費。
〔若有破損，請寄回更換，謝謝〕

國家圖書館出版品預行編目 (CIP) 資料

永恆的莎士比亞改寫劇本 .3：凱撒大帝 / William
Shakespeare, Brady Timoney 作 ; 蘇瑞琴譯 .-- 初版 .--
[臺北市]：寂天文化, 2016.08
面 ; 公分
ISBN 978-986-318-487-4(平裝附光碟片)

873.43358　　　　　　　　　　　　105014692

Contents

Introduction 🎧

It is 44 b.c. in Rome. Julius Caesar, an army general, has defeated a Roman aristocrat named Pompey in a fierce battle. A public celebration is being held as the play opens. But some of the noblemen who had supported Pompey are fearful of Caesar's growing popularity. They're afraid that the ambitious Caesar wants to be named king—which would mean the end of the great Roman Republic. To protect their own power, they begin to conspire against him.

Cast of Characters 🎧

JULIUS CAESAR Roman statesman and army general

OCTAVIUS A Roman politician; later called Augustus Caesar, first Emperor of Rome

MARK ANTONY A Roman politician, general, and friend of Caesar

LEPIDUS A Roman politician

MARCUS BRUTUS, CASSIUS, CASCA, TREBONIUS, LIGARIUS, DECIUS BRUTUS, METELLUS CIMBER, and **CINNA** Plotters against Caesar

CALPURNIA Caesar's wife

PORTIA Brutus's wife

CICERO, POPILIUS, and **POPILIUS LENA** Senators

FLAVIUS and **MARULLUS** Tribunes

CATO, LUCILIUS, TITINIUS, MESSALA, and **VOLUMNIUS**
Supporters of Brutus

ARTEMIDORUS A teacher of rhetoric

PUBLIUS An elderly gentleman

STRATO and **LUCIUS** Servants to Brutus

PINDARUS Servant to Cassius
THE GHOST OF CAESAR

A **SOOTHSAYER,** a **POET, SENATORS, CITIZENS, SOLDIERS,**
COMMONERS, MESSENGERS, and **SERVANTS**

ACT 1

Summary

弗拉維烏斯和馬魯路士非常憤怒,他們將等待擁戴凱撒凱旋羅馬的平民趕回家,並撤除榮耀凱撒的旗幟。

另一頭,凱撒和他的追隨者正在等待觀賞為牧神節而舉辦的賽事,一位占卜者從群眾中現身,要凱撒留心三月十五日。

布魯圖斯與喀西約談及布魯圖斯近日甚為心煩,喀西約暗示布魯圖斯比凱撒更適合當領導者,他談到凱撒的缺點與雄心抱負,說凱撒在馬克安東尼交付王冠給他時拒絕了三次。喀西約決心要改變布魯圖斯對凱撒的欽佩看法。

當晚,一場大暴風雨席捲羅馬,眾人看到了奇怪的景象。喀西約和喀司加用負面的口吻談論凱撒,喀西約邀請喀司加一同加入他與其他夥伴,參與一場對凱撒不利的陰謀。他們認為若布魯圖斯也願意加入他們的行列,行動成功的機率將大幅提高,喀西約和喀司加決定在翌日早晨再說服布魯圖斯。

Scene ❶

(A street in Rome. **Flavius**, **Marullus**, and certain **commoners** enter.)

FLAVIUS: Go home, you idle creatures!
　Is this a holiday? Don't you know you're
　Not allowed to walk around on a workday
　Without some sign of your profession?
　Tell me, what is your trade?

COMMONER 1: Why, sir, I am a carpenter.

MARULLUS: Where are your tools?
　Why are you wearing your best clothes?
　And you, sir—what is your trade?

COMMONER 2: Sir, I am a cobbler.
　I work with a clear conscience,
　For I am, sir, a mender of bad soles.
　If you are out of sorts, sir, I can mend you.

MARULLUS: What do you mean by that? Hmm.
　Mend *me*, you saucy fellow?

COMMONER 2: Why, sir—repair your shoes.

FLAVIUS: Why aren't you in your shop? Why do you
　lead these men about the streets?

COMMONER 2: To wear out their shoes, sir. Then I'll
get more work. But, indeed,
sir, we've taken a holiday to see Caesar and to
rejoice in his triumph.

MARULLUS: Why rejoice? What has he won?
What captives does he bring home?
You blocks, you stones, you worse than senseless
things!
Oh, you hard hearts, you cruel men of Rome!
Do you not remember Pompey? Many a
Time you've climbed up walls and towers,
Your infants in your arms. There you've sat
All day long, waiting patiently to
See great Pompey pass the streets of Rome.
And when you saw his chariot appear,
Didn't you shout so loud that the
River Tiber trembled under her banks
With the echo of your sounds?
And now you put on your best clothes?
You call out a holiday and
Lay flowers before him who comes
In triumph over Pompey's blood?
Be gone!

Run to your houses, fall upon your knees!
Beg the gods to stop the plague
That will surely punish you for such ingratitude.

FLAVIUS: Go, go, good countrymen—and,
For this fault, gather all the men like you.
Draw them to the banks of the Tiber, and
Weep into the river until the
Lowest stream kisses the highest shores.

(All the **commoners** exit.)

See how they vanish, silent in their guilt.
You go down that way toward the Capitol.
I'll go this way. Remove any banners
You see that honor Caesar.

MARULLUS: May we do so?
You know it is the feast of Lupercal.

FLAVIUS: It doesn't matter. Let no statues
Be hung with Caesar's trophies. I'll drive
The commoners from the streets.
You do the same, where you see them thick.
We must pluck these feathers from
Caesar's wing before he can soar so high
We'll have even more to fear.

(**Flavius** and **Marullus** exit.)

JULIUS CAESAR

Scene ❷ ⌒

(A public place. The sound of trumpets. **Caesar** enters, followed by **Antony**, **Calpurnia**, **Portia**, **Decius**, **Cicero**, **Brutus**, **Cassius**, and **Casca**. A **crowd** follows, among them a **soothsayer**.)

CAESAR: Calpurnia!

CALPURNIA: Here, my lord.

CAESAR: Stand directly in Antony's way,
When he runs his course. Antony!
Do not forget to touch Calpurnia
As you race past her. The elders say that
Childless women, touched in this holy race
On the feast of Lupercal, will soon be able
To have children.

ANTONY: I shall remember.
When Caesar says "Do this," it is performed.

(Trumpets sound.)

SOOTHSAYER (*from the crowd*): Caesar!
Beware the ides of March.

CAESAR: Who said that?

BRUTUS: A soothsayer warns you to be careful on
March 15.

10

CAESAR: Let me see his face.

CASSIUS: Fellow, come out of the crowd!

CAESAR: Speak once again.

SOOTHSAYER: Beware the ides of March.

CAESAR: He is a dreamer. Let us leave him.

(**All** but Brutus and Cassius exit.)

CASSIUS: Will you go watch the race?

BRUTUS: I am not interested in games. I lack
That quick spirit that is in Antony.
But don't let me stop you, Cassius.
I'll leave, and you can watch.

CASSIUS: Brutus, I have noticed that
You seem to be avoiding me lately.

BRUTUS: No, Cassius. It's just that I've been
Concerned with some personal matters.
But do not let my good friends—of which,
Cassius, you are one—worry too much about
me.
My neglect of friends is only because
Poor Brutus is at war with himself.

CASSIUS: Then I have been mistaken.
I have kept my thoughts to myself.
Tell me, good Brutus, can you see your face?

BRUTUS: No, for the eye does not see itself
Except by reflection in other things.

CASSIUS: It is very sad, Brutus,
That you have no mirrors to reveal
Your hidden worth to your own eyes.
I have heard many respected Romans,
Except immortal Caesar, praising you.
Groaning under these troubled times, they
Wish that noble Brutus had Caesar's eyes.

BRUTUS: Into what dangers would you lead me,
Cassius? Would you have me
Seek in myself that which is not there?

CASSIUS: Good Brutus,
Since you know you cannot see yourself
Except by reflection, let me be your mirror.
I will show you things about yourself
That you do not yet know.

(Trumpets and shouting from offstage.)

BRUTUS: What does this shouting mean?
I do fear the people are calling out for
Caesar to be their king.

CASSIUS *(slyly)*: Oh, do you fear it?
Then I must think you would not have it so.

BRUTUS: I would not—yet I love him well.
But why do you hold me here so long?
What is it that you want to say to me?
If it is not toward the general good,
Set honor in one eye and death in the other,
And I will look on both indifferently.
For let the gods be my witness that I love
The name of honor more than I fear death.

CASSIUS: I know that virtue to be in you,
   as well as I know your face.
Well, honor is the subject of my story.
I cannot tell what you and other men
May think of this life—but, for my part,
I would rather not live than to stand
In awe of one no better than myself.
I was born as free as Caesar, and so were you.
We both have eaten as well, and we can both
Endure the winter's cold as well as he.
Once, upon a raw and gusty day,
Caesar said to me, "Do you dare, Cassius,
To leap into the angry Tiber along with me
And swim across?" Upon the word,
Dressed as I was, I plunged in
And told him to follow. So indeed he did.
The wild river roared, and we fought it
With straining muscles and brave hearts.
But before we could get across,
Caesar cried, "Help me, Cassius, or I sink!"
So I carried the weary Caesar
From the waves of the Tiber. Now this man
   has become a god—and Cassius is

A wretched creature who must bow

If Caesar carelessly nods at him!

He had a fever when he was in Spain, and

How he shook when the fit was upon him!

It's true—this god did shake!

His coward lips lost their color, and

That eye whose glance awes the world

Lost its luster. I heard him groan. Yes,

And that tongue that gives fine speeches

Cried out, "Give me some drink,"

Like a sick girl. You gods! It amazes me

That such a weak man should

Command the respect of the entire world

And keep all the honors to himself.

(Shouts and trumpets from offstage.)

BRUTUS: The crowd shouts again!

I do believe they are cheering for some

New honors to be heaped on Caesar.

CASSIUS: Why, man, he strides the narrow world

Like a Colossus, while we petty men

Walk under his huge legs, peeping about

To find ourselves dishonorable graves!

Men at some time are masters of their fates.

15

The fault, dear Brutus, is not in our stars,
But in ourselves, that we are underlings.
"Brutus" and "Caesar" are just names.
Why should Caesar's name be more honored
   than yours?
Write them together—your name is as
   fair as his.
Speak them—yours sounds just as good.
Weigh them—yours is as heavy.
Now, in the names of all the gods at once,
Upon what meat does Caesar feed that
He has grown so great? These times are shamed!
Rome, you have lost the breed of noble bloods!
When, since the great flood, has an age
Had only one famous man?
When people talked of Rome, when
Could they ever say that her wide walls
Held but one man?
Can this truly be Rome,
If there is only one man in it?

BRUTUS: I know that you are my friend.
   I have thought about these things already.
   Let me consider what you have said.

For now I will listen to you patiently.
A proper time will come to hear and answer
  such high things.
Until then, noble friend, chew upon this:
Brutus would rather be a villager
Than to call himself a son of Rome now.
If Caesar becomes king,
I am afraid of the effect on Rome.

CASSIUS: I am glad that my weak words have
  Struck this much show of fire from Brutus.

(**Caesar** and his **attendants** enter again.)

BRUTUS: The games are done, and Caesar is
  returning.

CASSIUS: As they pass, catch Casca's sleeve.
  In his sour fashion, he will tell you
  What important things happened today.

BRUTUS: I will do so. But look, Cassius,
  An angry spot is glowing on Caesar's brow,
  Calpurnia's cheek is pale, and Cicero has
  That same look he gets when he is crossed.

CASSIUS: Casca will tell us what happened.

CAESAR: Antony!

ANTONY: Caesar?

CAESAR: Let the men around me be fat,
Sleek-headed men, who sleep at night.
That Cassius has a lean and hungry look.
He thinks too much. Such men are dangerous.

ANTONY: Fear him not, Caesar.
Cassius is not dangerous.
He is a noble Roman and well-respected.

CAESAR: I wish he were fatter! I fear him not—
Yet if I were to fear anyone, I should avoid
No man as much as
That thin Cassius. He reads too much.
He is a close observer, and seems to
Understand men's thoughts.
He loves no plays, as you do, Antony.
He hears no music. He seldom smiles.
And when he does, he smiles as if
He mocks himself and scorns the spirit
That could be moved to smile at anything.
Such men are never at heart's ease when
They see someone greater than themselves.
That's why they are very dangerous.
I'm telling you what is to be feared,

Not what I fear—for always I am Caesar.

Come on my right side, for this ear is deaf.

Now tell me truly what you think of him.

(Trumpets sound. **Caesar** and his **attendants** exit, except Casca.)

CASCA: You pulled me by the cloak. Do you wish to
   speak with me?

BRUTUS: Yes. Tell us what happened today
   That made Caesar look so sad.

CASCA: Why, you were with him, weren't you?

BRUTUS: If I were, I wouldn't be asking you.

CASCA: Why, a crown was offered to him.
   He pushed it off with the back of his hand,
   And then the crowd started shouting.

BRUTUS: What was the second noise for?

CASCA: Why, for that, too.

CASSIUS: They shouted three times. What was the
   last cry for?

CASCA: Why, for that, too.

BRUTUS: Was the crown offered three times?

CASCA: Yes, indeed, it was. And he pushed it off
   three times—each time more gently than

before. And each time, the rabble shouted louder.

CASSIUS: Who offered him the crown?

CASCA: Why, it was Antony.

BRUTUS: Tell us the manner of it, gentle Casca.

CASCA: I saw Mark Antony offer him a crown—yet it was not really a crown, but it was one of those coronets—and, as I told you, he pushed it off once. But for all that, to my thinking, he really wanted to take it. Then Antony offered it to him again, and again he pushed it off. But, to my thinking, he hated to take his fingers off it. Then Antony offered it a third time, and he pushed it off once more. As he refused it, the throng hooted and clapped their chapped hands. Then they threw up their sweaty nightcaps and uttered a cloud of stinking breath because the crown had been refused. The smell almost choked Caesar, for he swooned and fell down.

As for me, I dared not laugh for fear of opening my lips and receiving the bad air.

ACT 1 SCENE 2

CASSIUS: But, tell me, how did Caesar swoon?

CASCA: He fell right in the marketplace. He foamed at mouth and was speechless.

BRUTUS: He must have the falling sickness.

CASSIUS: No, Caesar doesn't have it. But you and I and honest Casca, we have the falling sickness.

CASCA: I don't know what you mean by that.
I only know that Caesar fell down.

BRUTUS: What did he say when he came to?

CASCA: Well, before he fell down, he saw that the common herd was glad he'd refused

the crown. So he offered them
his throat to cut. Then he fell. When
he came to himself again, he asked if
he had done or said anything strange.
He wanted them to think he fell because of his
illness. Three or four women nearby cried out,
"What a good soul!" and forgave him with all
their hearts.
But there's no need to pay attention
to them. If Caesar had stabbed their mothers,
they would have done no less!

BRUTUS: And then he came away, looking sad?

CASCA: Yes.

CASSIUS: Did Cicero say anything?

CASCA: Yes, he spoke Greek.

CASSIUS: What did he say?

CASCA: Those who understood him smiled at one
another and shook their heads. But for my own
part, it was Greek to me. And here's more news,
too. Marullus and Flavius, for pulling down
banners Praising Caesar, are put to silence.
Farewell now. More things happened,
but I can't remember them.

CASSIUS: Will you dine with me tonight, Casca?

CASCA: No, I have other plans.

CASSIUS: Will you dine with me tomorrow?

CASCA: Yes—if I'm still alive, and you still want to, and your dinner is worth eating.

CASSIUS: Very well. I will expect you.

CASCA: Do so. Farewell, both.

(**Casca** exits.)

BRUTUS: What a rude fellow Casca has become!
He was very clever when he went to school.

CASSIUS: He is still very clever in any
Bold or noble enterprise.
This rudeness is a sauce to his good wit.
It helps men digest his words
With better appetite.

BRUTUS: And so it is. For now, I will leave you.
Tomorrow, if you wish to speak with me,
I will come see you at home. Or, if you will,
I will wait for you at my house.

CASSIUS: I will. Until then, think of the world.

(**Brutus** exits.)

Well, Brutus, you are noble. Yet I see
That you might be swayed from honor.
Therefore, it is proper that noble minds
Keep always with other noble minds, for
Who is so firm that he cannot be seduced?
Caesar is hard on me—but he loves Brutus.
If I were Brutus now and he were Cassius,
He would not humor me. Tonight I will
Throw writings in at his windows,
As if they came from several citizens.
They will all express the high opinion
That Rome has of his name, and then
Briefly mention Caesar's ambition.
After this, let Caesar watch his ways,
For we will shake him, or see worse days.

(**Cassius** exits.)

Scene ③ ⟨5⟩

(A street in Rome. Thunder and lightning rumble and flash. **Casca** enters from one side, with his sword drawn. **Cicero** enters from the other side.)

CICERO: Good evening, Casca.

    Did you bring Caesar home?

    Why are you breathless,

    And why do you stare like that?

CASCA: Oh, Cicero, I have seen storms when

    The scolding winds have broken oak trees.

    I have seen the ocean swell and rage

    As high as the threatening clouds.

    But not until tonight, never until now,

    Did I see a storm dropping fire!

    Either there's a war raging in heaven,

    Or the world has angered the gods, and

    The gods have sent destruction.

CICERO: Why, what did you see?

CASCA: A common slave—you know him—

    Held up his left hand, which flamed

    Like twenty torches joined. Yet his hand

    Did not get burned! In addition—

I have not since put away my sword—
I met a lion roaming near the Capitol.
It gazed upon me and went on by!
And I saw a hundred ghastly women.
They swore they saw men on fire
Walking up and down the streets!
And yesterday the owl, that bird of night,
Sat at the marketplace at noon,
  howling and shrieking.
When such things happen, let no man say,
"There are the reasons. They are natural."
For I believe they are omens about our time.

CICERO: Indeed, it is a strange time. But these
Signs might not mean what you think.
Does Caesar come to the Capitol tomorrow?

CASCA: He does, for he told Antony
To give you that message.

CICERO: Good night, then, Casca.
This disturbed night is not fit to walk in.

CASCA: Farewell, Cicero.

(**Cicero** exits. **Cassius** enters.)

CASSIUS: Who's there?

CASCA: A Roman.

CASSIUS: Casca, by your voice.

CASCA: Your ear is good. What a night this is!

CASSIUS: I could name a man, Casca, who is
Most like this dreadful night. He thunders,
Flashes, opens graves, and roars
As that lion did in the Capitol today.
He is a man no mightier than you or me
In personal action. Yet he's as fearful
And powerful as these strange signs.

CASCA: You mean Caesar, don't you, Cassius?

CASSIUS: Let it be who it is. For Romans now
Are flesh and blood just like their ancestors.
But, woe to us! Our fathers' minds are dead,
And we are ruled with our mothers' spirits.
Our actions make us look womanish.

CASCA: Indeed they say the senators tomorrow
Mean to establish Caesar as king.
He shall wear his crown by sea and land
In every place but here in Italy.

CASSIUS: I know where I will wear this dagger then.
(He points his dagger at his own chest.)

Cassius will deliver Cassius from bondage.

By this, you gods, the weak are made most
strong.

By this, you gods, all tyrants are defeated.

No stony tower, no walls of beaten brass,

No airless dungeon, no strong links of iron

Can hold in the strength of spirit.

Life, being tired of these worldly bars,

Never lacks the power to end itself.

If I know this, let all the world know it!

That part of tyranny that I do bear,

I can shake off whenever I wish.

(Sounds of thunder.)

CASCA: So can I.

And so every slave in his own hand holds

The power to end his captivity.

CASSIUS: And why should Caesar be a tyrant?

Poor man! I know he would not be a wolf

Except that he sees the Romans are sheep.

You start a mighty fire with weak straws.

What trash is Rome, what rubbish,

When it serves as the fuel to light up

So vile a thing as Caesar? But, oh grief,
Where have you led me? Perhaps I speak so
Before a willing slave. If so, I know that
I must answer for it. But I am armed,
And dangers do not frighten me.

CASCA: You speak to Casca.
I'm no grinning tell-tale. I agree with you.

(They shake hands.)

Be firm in your cause.
I will set this foot of mine as far
As he who goes farthest.

CASSIUS: There's a bargain made.
Listen, Casca, I have already moved
Some of the noblest-minded Romans
To help me do something both
Honorable and dangerous. They're waiting
For me now. The work we are planning
Is like this fearful night—
Most bloody, fiery, and terrible.

(Cinna enters.)

CASCA: Stand close. Here comes one who's
in a hurry.

CASSIUS: It's Cinna. I know him by his walk.
He is a friend. Cinna, where are you going?

CINNA: To find you. Who's that?

CASSIUS: It is Casca, one who is with us.

CINNA: I am glad of it. What a fearful night!
Two or three of us have seen strange sights.

CASSIUS: Are the others waiting for me?

CINNA: Yes, they are. Oh, Cassius, if you could
Only win the noble Brutus to our side—

CASSIUS: Don't worry, good Cinna. Take this
Paper and put it where Brutus will find it.
Throw this other paper in at his window.
Set this last one up with wax on the
statue of old Brutus, his ancestor.
When you've done all this, meet us at the
Usual place. Are the others already there?

CINNA: All but Metellus Cimber, and he's gone
To seek you at your house. Well, I will go
And put these papers where you told me.

(**Cinna** exits.)

CASSIUS: Come, Casca, you and I will see Brutus at
His house before day. Three parts of him
Are ours already—and the whole man
Will be ours when we next meet.

CASCA: Oh, he sits high in the people's hearts!
That which would seem evil in us,
Will become virtue and worthiness
Once Brutus is associated with it.

CASSIUS: You have understood his worth very well
and our great need of him.
Let us go, for it is after 12. At dawn
We will awake him and make him ours.

(**Cassius** and **Casca** exit.)

ACT 2

Summary

布魯圖斯內心交戰,思考如何對羅馬才
是最好的選擇。他了解凱撒的野心十
分危險,於是決定除掉凱撒才對羅馬最有益處。

密謀者在早上拜會布魯圖斯,而布魯圖斯答應協助他們。布
魯圖斯否決密謀者想一併暗殺馬克安東尼的念頭,認為安東
尼沒了凱撒將不具威脅力。

在凱撒家中,他的妻子卡爾普尼亞試圖勸阻他出門前往朱
比特神殿,因她做了相關的噩夢,並相信夢境中充滿不祥的
預兆。為了安撫她,凱撒答應待在家中,但狄西厄斯布魯圖斯
卻又說服他出門,於是凱撒與密謀者一同前往朱比特神殿。

阿特米多拉斯在神殿附近等待,希望能藉機轉交一封信給
凱撒,他在信中警告凱撒要小心敵人。

Scene ❶ 🎧

(**Brutus** enters his garden with **Lucius**.)

BRUTUS: Bring a candle to my study, Lucius.
When it is lighted, come and call me here.

LUCIUS: I will, my lord.

(**Lucius** exits.)

BRUTUS *(aside)*: How to best serve Rome?
It must be by Caesar's death. For my part,
I have no personal cause to spurn him,
But what about the general good? He wants
To be crowned. The question is how
  that might change his nature.
The bright day that brings forth the snake
Requires careful walking. A crown
Will likely put a sting in him,
That, at his will, may become dangerous.
Greatness is abused when it separates
Remorse from power. I have never known
Caesar's feelings to take over his reason.
But it is common knowledge
That lowliness is young ambition's ladder.

While on that ladder, the climber looks up.
But once he reaches the highest rung,
He turns his back on the ladder,
Looks to the sky, and scorns the low rungs
By which he did climb. So Caesar may.
And, in case he may, we must prevent it.
Therefore, we think him as a serpent's egg.
Once hatched, it would grow to be deadly.
So we must kill him in the shell.

(**Lucius** enters again.)

LUCIUS: The candle is burning, sir.
While in your study, I found this paper.
It wasn't there earlier.
(Lucius gives Brutus the letter.)

BRUTUS: Isn't tomorrow the Ides of March?

LUCIUS: I do not know, sir.

BRUTUS: Look at the calendar and let me know.

(**Lucius** exits.)

BRUTUS: The meteors whizzing through the air
Give enough light to read by.
(He opens the letter and reads.)
"Brutus, you are sleeping. Awake and see

yourself! Speak, strike, help Rome! Brutus, you
are sleeping. Awake!"
Such hints have been often dropped
In my study window. Am I asked
To speak and strike? Oh, Rome,
I promise that I will help you!

(**Lucius** enters again.)

LUCIUS: Sir, tomorrow is March 15.

(Knocking is heard from offstage.)

BRUTUS: Good. Go answer the door.

(**Lucius** exits.)

Since Cassius first spoke against Caesar,
I have not slept.
Between the thought of a dreadful thing
And the first motion toward it,
Time is like a nightmare.
Spirit and body argue,
And the state of man, like a little kingdom,
Suffers then the nature of a revolt.

(**Lucius** enters again.)

LUCIUS: Cassius and some others are here.

BRUTUS: Do you know the others?

LUCIUS: Their faces are buried in their cloaks.

BRUTUS: Let them enter.

(**Lucius** exits.)

> They are the plotters. Oh, Conspiracy!
> Are you ashamed to show your face by night,
> When evils are most free? How, then, by day
> Will you find a cave dark enough
> To hide your shameful face? Seek none,
> Conspiracy. Hide in smiles and friendliness.

(The conspirators, **Cassius**, **Casca**, **Decius**, **Cinna**, **Metellus Cimber**, and **Trebonius**, enter.)

CASSIUS: Good day, Brutus. Did we wake you?

BRUTUS: I've been up. I was awake all night.
Do I know these men who are with you?

CASSIUS: Yes, every one—and each man here
Honors you. All of us wish
You had that same opinion of yourself
That every noble Roman has of you.

BRUTUS: They are all welcome here. Give me your
hands, one by one.

CASSIUS: Then let us swear our determination.

BRUTUS: No, not an oath.

What more do we need than our own cause
To push us onward? No bond is greater
Than Romans who have given their word.
We have said that this shall be,
    or we will fall for it.
Oaths are for priests, cowards, and
Suffering souls who welcome wrongs.
Do not stain the virtue of our cause
Nor the strength of our spirits by thinking
We need an oath. If one of us breaks
Our promise, every drop of blood spilled by a
    Roman is tainted.

CASSIUS: What of Cicero? Shall we ask him?

CASCA: Let us not leave him out.

METELLUS: Yes, let us have him! His silver hairs
Will buy us a good opinion.
It shall be said that his judgment ruled our
    hands.
Our wild youth will be overshadowed
By his age and dignity.

BRUTUS: Do not include him, for he will never
Follow anything other men have begun.

CASSIUS: Then leave him out.

DECIUS: Shall no man be touched but Caesar?

CASSIUS: Good point, Decius. I don't think that
Mark Antony, so well-loved by Caesar,
Should outlive Caesar. He is very shrewd,
And he could hurt us later. To prevent that,
Let Antony and Caesar fall together.

BRUTUS: It seems too bloody to cut off
The head and then hack the limbs.
For Antony is but a limb of Caesar.
Let us be sacrificers, but not butchers.
We all stand up against the spirit of Caesar,
And in the spirit of men there is no blood.
If only we could strike Caesar's spirit
And not harm the man. But, alas,
Caesar must bleed for it! And, gentle friends,
Let's kill him boldly, but not in anger.
Let's carve him as a dish fit for the gods,
Not slice him as meat fit for dogs.
This will make our cause seem necessary,
and not done out of envy.
Appearing this way to the common eyes,

We shall be called cleansers, not murderers.
As for Mark Antony—don't think of him.
He can do no more than Caesar's arm
When Caesar's head is off.

CASSIUS: Yet he could be dangerous,
For in the love he bears to Caesar—

BRUTUS: Good Cassius, do not fear him.
If he loves Caesar, all he can do is
Kill himself, and die for his grief.
But I don't think he will. He so greatly
Enjoys sports and happy company.

TREBONIUS: There's no reason to fear Antony.
Let him live, for he will laugh at this later.

(Clock strikes.)

BRUTUS: It is time to part.

CASSIUS: We still don't know if Caesar
Will come out today. Lately,
He has been superstitious.
The unusual terror of this night,
And the warning of the seers,
May keep him from the Capitol today.

39

DECIUS: Don't worry. I can talk him into it.
    He loves to hear that charging unicorns
    May be fooled by trees, bears by mirrors,
    Lions by nets, and men by flatterers.
    But when I tell him he hates flatterers,
    He says he does—being then most flattered.
    Let me work, for I know how to talk to him,
    And I will get him to come to the Capitol.

CASSIUS: And we will all be there to fetch him.

BRUTUS: By the eighth hour. Is that the time?

CINNA: At the latest, and do not fail.

METELLUS: Ligarius dislikes Caesar, who
    Raged at him for speaking well of Pompey.
    I wonder why none of you thought of him.

BRUTUS: Go get him, good Metellus.
    I can ask him to help us, too.

CASSIUS: The morning comes upon us. Brutus,
    We'll leave now. All of you remember what
    You said and show yourselves true Romans.

BRUTUS: Gentlemen, look fresh and happy!
    Don't let our faces show our purposes.
    We must be like actors.

And so, good morning to you all.

(**All** exit but **Brutus**.)

Boy! Lucius! Fast asleep? It is no matter.

Enjoy the honey-heavy dew of slumber.

You have no cares or troubles.

That is why you sleep so soundly.

(**Portia** enters.)

PORTIA: Brutus, my lord!

BRUTUS: Portia, why are you up so early?

PORTIA: I am worried about you, Brutus.

You haven't been yourself lately.

Please tell me the cause of your grief.

BRUTUS: I am not well in health, that's all.

PORTIA: What—is Brutus sick? Yet he will

Steal out of his warm bed to dare

The night air to make him worse?

No, my Brutus, something is on your mind,

And I have the right to know about it.

Upon my knees, I ask you, by our love,

To tell me what it is. What men have come to

you this night? I know there were six

41

Or seven of them, who hid their faces
Even from darkness.

BRUTUS: Kneel not, gentle Portia.

PORTIA: I wouldn't need to if you were yourself,
gentle Brutus.

(A knocking is heard from offstage.)

BRUTUS: Someone knocks. Go inside awhile.
Later, I shall tell you the secrets of my heart.

(**Portia** exits. **Lucius** enters with **Ligarius**.)

BRUTUS: Caius Ligarius, how are you?
(to Lucius): Boy, stand aside.

(**Lucius** exits.)

LIGARIUS: I understand that you have in mind
A job worthy of the name of honor.

BRUTUS: I do indeed, Ligarius.

LIGARIUS: Soul of Rome! Brave son of
Honorable parents! You have revived
My unhappy spirit. What's to do?

BRUTUS: Work that will make sick men whole.

LIGARIUS: But are not some whole that should be
made sick?

BRUTUS: We must see to that. What it is,
My Caius, I shall tell you as we are going
To the place it must be done.

LIGARIUS: Lead the way. With all my heart,
I follow you—to do I know not what.
It is enough that Brutus leads me on.

BRUTUS: Follow me, then.

(**Brutus** and **Ligarius** exit.)

Scene ❷ ⌒₇

(Caesar's house. Thunder and lightning. **Caesar** enters, in his nightgown.)

CAESAR: Neither heaven nor earth has been
  At peace tonight. Three times,
  Calpurnia cried out in her sleep,
  "Help! They murder Caesar!"—Who's there?

(A **servant** enters.)

SERVANT: My lord?

CAESAR: Tell the priests to make a sacrifice,
  And bring me their opinions of success.

SERVANT: I will, my lord.

(**Servant** exits. **Calpurnia** enters.)

CALPURNIA: What do you mean, Caesar?
  Do you think you are going out?
  You shall not leave the house today!

CAESAR: Caesar shall go out. They who
  Threatened me looked only on my back.
  When they see my face, they will vanish.

CALPURNIA: I have never believed in omens,
  Yet now they frighten me. They say that

A lioness gave birth in the streets of Rome.

Last night, graves opened and gave up their
  dead.

Fierce fiery warriors fought upon the clouds,

In ranks and squadrons.

Blood drizzled upon the Capitol,

The noise of battle filled the air,

Horses neighed and dying men groaned,

And ghosts shrieked in the streets.

Oh, Caesar! These things are strange,

And I do fear them.

CAESAR: What can be avoided

If the mighty gods want it to happen?

Yet Caesar shall go forth, for these omens

May be for anyone, as well as for Caesar.

CALPURNIA: When beggars die, there are no comets
  seen.

The heavens themselves blaze forth only for the
  death of princes.

CAESAR: Cowards die many times before their
  deaths;

The valiant never taste of death but once.

Of all the wonders that I've yet heard,

It seems most strange that men fear death.

Since death is a necessary end,

It will come when it will come.

(**Servant** enters again.)

What do the priests say?

SERVANT: That you should not go out today.

When they sacrificed an animal,

The heart could not be found within

the beast!

CAESAR: The gods do this to shame cowardice.

Caesar would be a beast without a heart

If he stayed at home out of fear.

No, Caesar shall not. Danger knows full well

That Caesar is more dangerous than he!

We are like two lions from the same litter,

But I am the elder and more terrible.

So Caesar shall go forth.

CALPURNIA: Alas, my lord!

Your wisdom is eaten up by your confidence.

Do not go out today. Call it my fear and

Not your own that keeps you in the house!

We'll send Mark Antony to the Senate,

He'll say you are not well today.

Let me, upon my knees, have my way in this.

   (She kneels.)

ACT 2 SCENE 2

CAESAR: Mark Antony shall say I am not well,

And, to humor you, I will stay at home. *(Caesar lifts Calpurnia up.)*

(**Decius** enters.)

Here's Decius Brutus. He shall tell them so.

DECIUS: Good morning, worthy Caesar!

I come to bring you to the Senate House.

CAESAR: And you are just in time

To bring my greeting to the senators,

And tell them that I will not come today.

"Cannot" is false; "I dare not," even falser.

I will not come today. Tell them so, Decius.

CALPURNIA: Say that he is sick.

CAESAR: Shall Caesar send a lie?

Have I stretched my arm so far in conquest

To fear telling graybeards the truth?

Decius, go tell them Caesar will not come.

DECIUS: Most mighty Caesar, tell me why—

So I won't be laughed at when I tell them so.

47

CAESAR: It is my will. I will not come.

That is enough to satisfy the Senate.

But, just between us, I will let you know.

Calpurnia wants me to stay at home.

She dreamed last night she saw my statue,

Which, like a fountain with 100 spouts,

Ran with pure blood. Many joyful Romans

Came smiling and bathed their hands in it.

She sees this as a warning and omen

Of evil. On her knees she has begged

That I stay home today.

DECIUS: But this dream means something else!

It was a vision fair and fortunate.

Your statue spouting blood from many pipes,

In which so many smiling Romans bathed,

Means that your blood will revive Rome.

Many great men shall come to you for

Your blessings and recognition.

This is what Calpurnia's dream means.

CAESAR: And you have said it well.

DECIUS: I have something else to say.

The Senate has decided to give a crown

To mighty Caesar this day. If you say you

Will not come, their minds may change.

Besides, it seems a mockery to say,

"The Senate can wait until another time—when
   Caesar's wife

Shall have better dreams."

If Caesar hides himself, won't they whisper,

"Caesar is afraid"?

Pardon me, Caesar, for saying all this,

But my love for you forces me to do so.

CAESAR: How foolish your fears seem now,
   Calpurnia!

I am ashamed I gave in to them.

Give me my robe, for I must go.

(**Publius**, **Brutus**, **Ligarius**, **Metellus**, **Casca**,
Trebonius, and **Cinna** enter.)

And here is Publius to bring me there.

PUBLIUS: Good morning, Caesar.

CAESAR: Welcome, Publius. What, Brutus,
   Are you up so early too? Good morning,
   Casca, and all of you. What time is it?

BRUTUS: Caesar, it is just past eight.

JULIUS CAESAR

CAESAR: I thank you all for coming for me.

(**Antony** enters.)

See, even Antony, who stays out late, is up.
Good morning, Antony.

ANTONY: The same to most noble Caesar.

CAESAR *(to a servant)*: Go inside.
Tell them to prepare some refreshments.
Now, Cinna, Metellus, and Trebonius,
Be near me, so I can talk to you.

TREBONIUS: Caesar, I will.
(aside): Yes, so near will I be that your
Best friends shall wish I had been further.

CAESAR: Friends, taste some wine with me.
Then, as friends, we'll go together after.

BRUTUS *(aside)*: Your so-called friends
Are not true. Oh, Caesar!
The heart of Brutus is saddened.

(**All** exit.)

Scene ❸ 🎧

(A street near the Capitol. **Artemidorus** enters, reading a paper.)

ARTEMIDORUS: "Caesar, beware of Brutus, Cassius, and Casca. Watch out for Cinna. Don't trust Trebonius. Avoid Metellus. Decius is not your friend, and neither is Ligarius. There is but one mind in all these men—and it is bent against Caesar. If you fear death, look around you! Thinking you're safe makes a conspiracy easier. May the mighty gods defend you! Your friend, Artemidorus."

I will stand here until Caesar passes by.

As a citizen I will give him this.

My heart aches that virtue cannot live
   out of envy's reach.

If you read this, Caesar, you may live.

If not, the fates are working with the traitors.

(**Artemidorus** exits.)

ACT 3

Summary

阿特米多拉斯無法在凱撒進入朱比特神殿之前給他警告信，就在元老院開議不久後，密謀者行刺凱撒得逞，最後一位行刺者是布魯圖斯。垂死的凱撒轉向布魯圖斯，對他說：「Et tu, Brutè?（你也是嗎，布魯圖斯？）」

密謀者開始擔心將如何為自己的行為向羅馬人民解釋，而安東尼要求與密謀者會面，了解凱撒必死的原因，布魯圖斯向安東尼擔保會面時的安危。在會面時，安東尼請求密謀者讓他在凱撒的葬禮上致詞，密謀者同意他的請求，但要求安東尼要在布魯圖斯演說後才能致詞。

密謀者離開後，安東尼差派僕人去找屋大維，他在羅馬二十哩遠之處帶兵紮營。安東尼的訊息中透露羅馬因凱撒遇刺一事，目前太危險，不適合屋大維前來。

在公共廣場上，布魯圖斯向群眾發言，告訴他們刺殺凱撒的原因，隨後安東尼帶著凱撒的遺體抵達。當安東尼發表演說時，群眾從同情布魯圖斯轉為同情安東尼，特別在安東尼朗誦凱撒遺言之後更是如此。群眾決定要為凱撒之死復仇，有些人甚至跑走，打算燒毀叛徒的房舍。

Scene ❶ 🎧

(Rome, in front of the Capitol. A crowd, including Artemidorus and the soothsayer, awaits. Trumpets sound. **Caesar, Brutus, Cassius, Casca, Decius, Metellus, Trebonius, Cinna, Antony, Lepidus, Popilius, Publius,** and **others** enter.)

CAESAR: The ides of March have come.

SOOTHSAYER: Yes, Caesar—but not gone.

ARTEMIDORUS (*offering his letter*): Hail, Caesar! Read this!

DECIUS: Trebonius wishes you to read,
At your convenience, his humble suit.

ARTEMIDORUS: Oh, Caesar, read mine first,
For mine concerns you more closely.
Read it without delay, great Caesar.

CAESAR: What concerns me shall be read last.

ARTEMIDORUS: Don't wait, Caesar. Read it instantly.

CAESAR: What, is this fellow mad?

PUBLIUS: Sir, step aside.

CASSIUS: Why do you urge your suit here,
Artemidorus? Come to the Capitol.

(**Caesar** goes forward, the rest following.)

POPILIUS *(to Cassius)*: Good luck today.

CASSIUS: With what, Popilius?

POPILIUS: Farewell.

(**Popilius** advances toward **Caesar**.)

BRUTUS: What did Popilius say?

CASSIUS: He wished me good luck.
I fear our plot has been discovered!

BRUTUS: Look, he goes to Caesar. Watch him.

CASSIUS: Brutus, what shall we do?

BRUTUS: Cassius, calm down.
Popilius is not telling Caesar of our plan.
He's smiling, and Caesar is not troubled.

CASSIUS: Trebonius is ready. Look—
He draws Mark Antony out of the way.

(**Antony** and **Trebonius** exit.)

DECIUS: Where is Metellus Cimber? It's time
For him to present his suit to Caesar.

CINNA: Casca, you must raise your hand first.

(They enter the Senate House.)

CAESAR: Are we all ready? What problems
Must Caesar and his Senate consider?

METELLUS *(kneeling)*: Most mighty Caesar,
Metellus Cimber throws his heart before you.

CAESAR: I must stop you, Cimber. These bows
Might move ordinary men to change the laws,
but they don't move me.
Your brother has been banished for a reason.
If you bow and pray and beg for him,
I will kick you out of my way like a dog.
Know that Caesar does not act unjustly.
He will not change his mind without
just cause.

METELLUS: Is there no voice more worthy than
My own to speak for my banished brother?

BRUTUS *(kneeling)*: I kiss your hand—
But not in flattery, Caesar. I ask that
Publius Cimber be allowed to come home.

CAESAR: What, Brutus?

CASSIUS *(kneeling)*: Pardon, Caesar!
Caesar, pardon! I fall as low as your foot
To beg for Publius Cimber's pardon.

CAESAR: I could be moved by this—
If I were like you. If I could beg others,

Begging would move me.

But I am constant as the northern star,

Which is unlike all other stars in the sky.

The skies are painted with a million sparks.

All are fire and every one does shine,

  but only one holds its place.

The world is the same. It is full of men.

The men are flesh and blood, and worried.

Yet of all those men, I know only one

Who keeps his strong position.

He does not move. I am that one.

Let me show it, even in this.

I was firm that Publius Cimber be banished.

I remain firm to keep him so.

CINNA *(kneeling)*: Oh, Caesar—

CAESAR: Away! Do you think you can lift Olympus?

DECIUS *(kneeling)*: Great Caesar—

CASCA: Speak, hands, for me!

(Casca stabs Caesar. The others also rise up and stab Caesar. Brutus is last.)

CAESAR: *Et tu, Brutè?* Then fall, Caesar!

(**Caesar** dies.)

CINNA: Liberty! Freedom! Tyranny is dead!

Run, announce it! Cry it in the streets!

BRUTUS: People and senators, do not fear.

Don't run. Be still. Ambition's debt is paid.

CASCA: Go to the pulpit, Brutus.

DECIUS: And Cassius, too.

BRUTUS: Where's Publius?

CINNA: Here, and quite confused by all this.

METELLUS: Stand close together, ready to fight,
  In case some friend of Caesar's
    should happen to—

BRUTUS: Don't talk of fighting.
  Publius, don't worry.
  We will not harm you or any other Roman.

CASSIUS: Go tell them, Publius. And take care
  That the people rushing at us don't hurt you.

BRUTUS: Poor, confused Publius! Let no man pay for
  this but us, the doers.

(**Trebonius** enters again.)

CASSIUS: Where is Antony?

TREBONIUS: Fled to his house, stunned.
  Men, wives, and children stare, cry out, and
  Run as if the world were coming to an end.

BRUTUS: Fates, we will soon know your wish!
  We know that we shall die. It's only the
  Time of our death we don't know.

CASSIUS: Why, he that cuts off 20 years of life
  Cuts off so many years of fearing death.

BRUTUS: That being so, then we are
Caesar's friends, who have cut short his time
Of fearing death. Stoop, Romans, stoop,
And let us bathe our hands in Caesar's blood
Up to the elbows, and smear our swords.
Then let's walk out, even to the marketplace.
Waving our red weapons over our heads,
Let's all cry, "Peace, freedom, and liberty!"

CASSIUS: Stoop then, and wash!

(They smear their hands and swords with Caesar's blood.)

How many ages in the future
Shall our great scene be acted over
In states unborn and accents yet unknown!
As often as that shall be,
That is how often we shall be called
The men who gave their country liberty.

DECIUS: What now? Shall we go?

CASSIUS: Yes, every man.
Brutus shall lead, and we will follow—
The boldest and best hearts of Rome.

(Antony's **servant** enters.)

BRUTUS: Wait, who's coming? A friend of Antony's?

SERVANT *(kneeling):* Like this, Brutus, my master
said to kneel.
And he told me what to say:
Brutus is noble, wise, brave, and honest.
Caesar was mighty, bold, royal, and loving.
Say I love Brutus and I honor him.
Say I feared, honored, and loved Caesar.
If Brutus will let Antony come to him
In safety,
And hear why Caesar deserved to die,
He will show Brutus due respect and
Love him living more than Caesar dead.
He will follow Brutus in his new role, with
All true faith. So says my master Antony.

BRUTUS: Your master is wise and valiant.
I never thought him worse.
Tell him to come here, if he pleases.
He shall have what he asks—and,
By my honor, he shall leave unharmed.

SERVANT: I'll get him now.

(**Servant** exits.)

BRUTUS: I know that he will be a friend.

CASSIUS: I hope so, yet my mind fears him.

(**Antony** enters again.)

BRUTUS: Here he is. Welcome, Mark Antony.

ANTONY *(seeing the body)*: Oh, mighty Caesar!
Do you lie so low?
Are all your conquests, glories, triumphs,
Shrunk to this small size? Farewell!
I don't know, gentlemen, what you intend.
Who else must die? If I myself, there is no
Better hour than Caesar's hour of death,
And no weapons worth half as much
As your swords, made rich
With the most noble blood of all this world.
I beg you, if you think I am your enemy,
To do what you wish now, while your
Bloody hands still reek and smoke.
If I live a thousand years,
I shall not find a better time and place to die,
Than here, by Caesar, and cut off by you,
The choice and master spirits of our age.

BRUTUS: Antony, don't beg your death from us!

I know we must appear bloody and cruel.

You see our hands and this,

(pointing to Caesar's body):

The bleeding business they have done.

You do not see our hearts, full of pity.

But as fire drives out fire,

So one pity drives out another.

Our pity for the wrongs Rome has suffered

Has done this deed to Caesar. But for you,

Mark Antony, our swords have blunt points.

Our arms and our hearts do receive you

With nothing but kind love and respect.

CASSIUS: You will have as strong a voice

As any man in choosing our new leaders.

BRUTUS: Just be patient until we've quieted

The people, now filled with fear.

Then I will tell you why I,

Who did love Caesar when I struck him,

Did what had to be done.

ANTONY: I don't doubt your wisdom.

Let each man give me his bloody hand.

I wish to shake each one.

(They all shake hands.)

Gentlemen, what can I say?
You must see me in one of two bad ways—
Either as a coward or a flatterer.
That I did love you, Caesar, oh, it is true!
If your spirit looks upon us now,
It must grieve you more than your death
To see your Antony making his peace,
Shaking the bloody hands of your foes
In the presence of your corpse.
If I had as many eyes as you have wounds,
Crying as fast as they stream out your blood,
It would become me better than meeting
Your enemies in friendship.
Pardon me, Julius!
Here you were surrounded, brave deer!
Here you fell, and here your hunters
Stand covered in your blood.
Oh, world, you were the forest to this deer,
And this, indeed, oh, world,
Was the heart of you.
How like a deer struck by many princes
Do you here lie!

CASSIUS: Mark Antony, I don't blame you for
   praising Caesar.
   But what does it mean?
   Can we still count on you as a friend?

ANTONY: That's why I took your hands.
   I was only swayed for a moment
   By looking down at Caesar.
   I love you all and will be your friend—
   If you give me reasons why, and
   In what ways, Caesar was dangerous.

BRUTUS: Our reasons are so good, Antony,
   That even if you were Caesar's son,
   You would be satisfied.

ANTONY: That's all I seek.
   And I also ask to bring his body
   To the marketplace so that,
   As a friend, I may speak at his funeral.

BRUTUS: You shall, Mark Antony.

CASSIUS: Brutus, a word with you.
   (aside to Brutus): Think again about that.
   If Antony speaks at his funeral,
   Do you know how deeply the people

Will be moved by his words?

BRUTUS *(aside to Cassius)*: I'll speak first
And tell them why Caesar had to die.
They'll know that Antony speaks by
Our permission, and that we want Caesar
To have all the honors the dead deserve.
It shall help us more than hurt us.

CASSIUS: I still don't like the idea.

BRUTUS: Mark Antony, take Caesar's body.
You shall not in your speech blame us,
But say all the good you can of Caesar.
Say you speak by our permission—
Or you shall not have anything to do
With his funeral. And you shall speak
From the same pulpit that I do,
After my speech is ended.

ANTONY: I desire no more than that.

BRUTUS: Prepare the body, then, and follow us.

(**All** exit but **Antony**.)

ANTONY: Oh, forgive me, you bleeding piece of earth,
That I am meek and gentle with these butchers!
You are the ruins of the noblest man

That ever lived in the tide of times.
Woe to the hand that shed this costly blood!
A curse shall fall upon the limbs of men.
Violent civil war shall shake Italy.
Blood and cruelty will become so common that
Mothers will but smile when they see their
Infants cut to pieces by the hands of war.
Caesar's spirit, eager for revenge,
Shall, with a king's voice, cry "Havoc!"
And let slip the dogs of war.
This foul deed will smell above the earth
While rotting corpses beg to be buried.

(Octavius's **servant** enters.)

You serve Octavius Caesar, do you not?

SERVANT: I do, Mark Antony.

ANTONY: Caesar asked him to come to Rome.

SERVANT: Lord Octavius got Caesar's letters
And is on his way. He told me to tell you—
(He sees the body.) Oh, Caesar!

ANTONY: Your heart is big. Go away and cry.
Sorrow, I see, is catching—for my eyes,
Seeing those beads of sorrow in yours,
Began to water. Where is your master?

SERVANT: He camps just 20 miles from Rome.

ANTONY: Go and report what has happened.
It is too dangerous for him here.
Go back and tell him so—but stay awhile.
Help me take the body to the marketplace.
I will make a speech and see how the people
React to what these bloody men have done.
Now lend me your hand.
Then go tell Octavius the state of things.

(**Antony** and **servant** exit with **Caesar's body.**)

Scene ❷ 🎧

(The Forum. **Brutus** and **Cassius** enter, along with a **crowd of citizens**.)

CITIZENS: We will be satisfied!

BRUTUS: Then listen to me, friends.

I will tell you the reasons for Caesar's death.

(**Brutus** goes to the pulpit.)

CITIZEN 1: Brutus will speak. Silence!

BRUTUS: Be patient until the end. Romans, countrymen, and friends! Be silent, so you may hear my words. Believe me because of my honor, and have respect for my honor, so you may believe. Judge me by your wisdom, and awaken your senses so you may judge wisely. If anyone in this crowd was a friend of Caesar's, I say to him that Brutus's love of Caesar was no less than his. If that friend asks why Brutus rose against Caesar, this is my answer: Not that I loved Caesar less, but that I loved Rome more. Would you rather that Caesar were living, and we all died slaves? Or would you rather

have Caesar dead, and live as free men? As
Caesar loved me, I weep for him.

As he was lucky, I rejoice for him. As he was
brave, I honor him. But as he was ambitious—I
killed him. Who here is so low that he would
be a slave? If any, speak out, for I have offended
him. Who here is so vile that he will not
love his country? If any, speak out, for I have
offended him. I pause for a reply.

ACT 3
SCENE 2

ALL: None, Brutus, none.

BRUTUS: Then none have I offended.

(**Antony** and **others** enter, with **Caesar's body**.)

Here comes his body, mourned by Mark
Antony, who had no hand in his death, but
shall receive benefit from it. He, like all of you,
shall have a place in the ruling of our country.
With this I end: As I killed my best friend
for the good of Rome, I have the same dagger
for myself when it shall please my country to
require my death.

ALL: Live, Brutus, live, *live*!

CITIZEN 1: Bring him to his house with honor.

CITIZEN 2: Give him a statue.

CITIZEN 3: Let him be Caesar.

CITIZEN 4: Caesar's better parts
Shall be crowned in Brutus.

BRUTUS: My countrymen—

CITIZEN 2: Peace! Silence! Brutus speaks.

BRUTUS: Good people, allow me to leave alone.

For my sake, stay here with Antony,

Honor Caesar's corpse, and hear the speech

Which, by our permission, Mark Antony

Is allowed to make. I beg you, no one leave,

Except me, until Antony has spoken.

(**Brutus** exits.)

CITIZEN 1: Let us hear Mark Antony.

CITIZEN 3: Yes! Let him go up into the pulpit.

We'll hear him. Noble Antony, go up!

ANTONY: For Brutus's sake, I owe this to you.

(**Antony** goes to the pulpit.)

CITIZEN 4: What did he say about Brutus?

CITIZEN 3: For Brutus's sake, he owes us.

CITIZEN 4: It would be best that he speak no harm of

Brutus here.

CITIZEN 1: This Caesar was a tyrant.

CITIZEN 3: Yes, that's certain.

We are blessed that Rome is rid of him.

ANTONY: You gentle Romans—

ALL: Quiet! Let us hear him.

ANTONY: Friends, Romans, countrymen, lend me
  your ears!
I come to bury Caesar, not to praise him.
The evil that men do lives after them,
The good is often buried with their bones.
So let it be with Caesar. The noble Brutus
Has told you Caesar was ambitious.
If it were so, it was a serious fault,
And seriously has Caesar answered for it.
Here, by permission of Brutus and the rest—
For Brutus is an honorable man;
So are they all, all honorable men—
I come to speak at Caesar's funeral.
He was my friend, faithful and just to me.
But Brutus says he was ambitious,
And Brutus is an honorable man.
Caesar brought many captives to Rome,
Whose ransoms filled the public treasury.
Did this in Caesar seem ambitious?
When the poor have cried, Caesar has wept.
Ambition should be made of sterner stuff.
Yet Brutus says he was ambitious,

And Brutus is an honorable man.

You all saw, on the feast of Lupercal,

Three times I presented him a kingly crown,

Which he three times refused. Was this
    ambition?

Yet Brutus says he was ambitious,

And surely he is an honorable man.

I speak not to disprove what Brutus said,

But only to speak of what I do know.

All of you loved Caesar at one time,
    not without cause.

What cause now stops you, then,
    from mourning for him?

Oh judgment, you have fled to brutish beasts,

And men have lost their reason!

(He cries.) Bear with me.

My heart is in the coffin there with Caesar,

And I must pause until it returns to me.

CITIZEN 1: I think he makes a lot of sense.

CITIZEN 2: You heard his words?

Caesar would not take the crown.

Therefore, it is certain he was not ambitious.

CITIZEN 3: It seems Caesar has been wronged.

CITIZEN 4: If so, someone must pay for it!

CITIZEN 2: Poor Antony! Look—his sore eyes are as red as fire with weeping.

CITIZEN 3: There's not a nobler man in Rome than Antony.

CITIZEN 4: Listen. He begins again to speak.

ANTONY: Only yesterday Caesar's word
 Stood against the world. Now here he lies.
 Where is proper respect?
 Oh, masters! If I wanted to stir your rage,
 I would do Brutus and Cassius wrong,
 Who, you all know, are honorable men.
 I will not do them wrong. I would prefer to
 Wrong the dead, to wrong myself and you,
 Than to wrong such honorable men.
 But here's a paper with the seal of Caesar.
 I found it in his closet. It is his will.
 If the common people heard it, they would
 Rush to kiss dead Caesar's wounds and
 Dip their handkerchiefs in his blood—
 Yes, and beg a hair of his for memory and,
 Dying, mention it in their wills, passing it on
 As a rich treasure to their children.

CITIZEN 4: Read the will, Mark Antony!

ALL: The will! Let's hear Caesar's will.

ANTONY: Patience, friends, I must not read it.
 You are not wood, not stones, but men.
 Hearing the will of Caesar will inflame you.

It will make you mad. It is good that
You don't know that you are his heirs,
For if you did, then what would come of it?

CITIZEN 4: Read the will. We'll hear it, Antony.

ANTONY: I've gone too far to tell you of it.
I fear I wrong the honorable men
Whose daggers have stabbed Caesar.

CITIZEN 4: Traitors all, not honorable men!

ALL: The will! The testament!

CITIZEN 2: They were villains, murderers!
The will! Read the will!

ANTONY: You will force me then to read it?
Make a ring around the corpse of Caesar,
Look closely at him who made the will.
Shall I come down? Have I your permission?

ALL: Come down!

(**Antony** comes down from the pulpit.)

CITIZEN 3: Make a ring. Gather around.

CITIZEN 4: Stand back from the body.

CITIZEN 2: Make room for the noble Antony.

ANTONY: If you have tears, prepare to shed them
  now.
  You all know this cloak. I remember
  The first time Caesar ever wore it.
  It was on a summer's evening, in his tent,
  On a day he won a great battle.
  Look, in this place ran Cassius's dagger.
  See what a tear the envious Casca made,
  And here his best friend Brutus stabbed.
  As he pulled his cursed steel away,
  See how the blood of Caesar followed it,
  As if rushing outside to see for sure
  If Brutus so unkindly knocked, for
  Brutus, as you know, was Caesar's angel.
  Oh, you gods, how dearly Caesar loved him!
  This was the unkindest cut of all.
  For when the noble Caesar saw him stab,
  It burst his mighty heart. Great Caesar fell.
  Oh, what a fall there was, my countrymen!
  Then I, and you, and all of us fell down,
  While bloody treason rose up over us.
  Oh, now you weep, and I know that you feel

The force of pity. These are gracious drops.
Kind souls, why do you weep when
All you see is Caesar's wounded clothing?
Look here. *(He lifts Caesar's cloak.)*
Here is the man himself—
Stabbed, you see, by traitors.

CITIZEN 1: Oh, pitiful sight!

CITIZEN 2: Oh, noble Caesar!

CITIZEN 3: Oh, day of woe!

CITIZEN 4: Oh, most bloody sight!

CITIZEN 1: We will get our revenge.

ALL: Revenge! Let's find them! Burn!
Kill! Let not a traitor live!

ANTONY: Stay, countrymen.

CITIZEN 1: Quiet, there! Hear the noble Antony.

CITIZEN 2: We'll hear him, we'll follow him, we'll die
with him!

ANTONY: Good friends, let me not stir you up.
They who have done this deed are honorable.
I do not know what made them do it.
As they are wise and honorable, they

Will, no doubt, give you good reasons.
I did not come to steal away your hearts.
I am no fine speaker, as Brutus is.
As you all know, I am a plain, blunt man
Who loved my friend. My poor words
Only tell you what you already know.
I must ask these wounds,
    poor dumb mouths,
To speak for me. But if I were Brutus, and
Brutus were Antony, there would be an
Antony who would stir your spirits until
Every wound of Caesar would cry out,
And move the very stones of Rome to rise and
    mutiny.

ALL: We'll have revenge!

CITIZEN 1: We'll burn the house of Brutus!

CITIZEN 3: Let's go. Seek the conspirators!

ANTONY: Please let me speak, countrymen.
    You have forgotten the will I mentioned.

ALL: The will! Let's stay and hear the will.

ANTONY: Here is the will, under Caesar's seal.
    It grants every Roman citizen 75 drachmas.

CITIZEN 2: Noble Caesar! We'll avenge you!

ANTONY: He's also left you all his walks,
His private arbors, and new-planted orchards
Along the Tiber River. He has left them
For you and your heirs to enjoy forever.
Here was a Caesar! When comes another like
him?

CITIZEN 1: Never, never! Come, away, away!
We'll burn his body in the holy place,
And with the burning sticks set fire
To the traitors' houses. Take up the body!

CITIZEN 2: Go fetch fire.

CITIZEN 3: Tear down their houses, benches,
windows—everything!

(**Citizens** exit with **the body.**)

ANTONY: Now let it work.
Trouble, you're loose. Go where you want.

(A **servant** enters.)

What is it, fellow?

SERVANT: Sir, Octavius is in Rome.
He and Lepidus are at Caesar's house.

ANTONY: I'll go straight there.

SERVANT: He said that Brutus and Cassius
Rode like madmen away from Rome.

ANTONY: They probably heard about how I had
Moved the people. Bring me to Octavius.

(**They** exit.)

ACT 3
SCENE
2

ACT 4

Summary

不久之後，安東尼、屋大維和雷比達會
面，並商討要殺死哪些密謀者。

布魯圖斯與其他密謀者已離開羅馬，目前與其軍隊在希臘紮
營。布魯圖斯和喀西約爭執後又和好，布魯圖斯告訴喀西約
他接到波西亞去世的噩耗，她因過度憂傷而自殺。

一位使者抵達通報消息，屋大維和馬克安東尼帶領千軍萬馬
要對付他們。密謀者開始計畫抵禦的方式，他們決定行軍至
腓立比與之交鋒。

當晚，凱撒的鬼魂在布魯圖斯的營帳中顯靈，鬼魂告訴布魯
圖斯，他倆將在腓立比相會。

Scene ❶ 🎧

(A house in Rome. Antony, Octavius, and Lepidus are seated at a table.)

ACT 4
SCENE
1

ANTONY: All of these conspirators shall die. Their
names are marked.

OCTAVIUS: Your brother must die, too. Do you agree,
Lepidus?

LEPIDUS: I do agree. On one condition—Publius,
Your sister's son, shall also die.

ANTONY: Agreed. Look, I mark his name, too.
Now, Lepidus, go to Caesar's house.
Get the will, so we can figure out
How to reduce the amount he left the people.

(**Lepidus** exits.)

ANTONY: There goes an unimportant man,
Fit to be sent on errands. Is it right that he
Should share power equally with us?

OCTAVIUS: You thought so when you took his
Advice about who should live and die.

ANTONY: Octavius, I have seen more days
Than you. We lay these honors on this man

To ease ourselves of some of the blame.

He'll carry them as a donkey carries gold,

Groaning and sweating under the load,

Either led or driven, as we point the way.

When he takes our treasure where we want,

We will take down his load and turn him out
  like a donkey,

To shake his ears and graze in the pastures.

OCTAVIUS: You may do as you please,

But he's a proven and brave soldier.

ANTONY: So is my horse, Octavius—and for that

I give him hay. He's a creature that I teach

To fight, to turn, to stop, to go ahead.

His body is controlled by my spirit.

In some ways, Lepidus is just like that.

Think of him only as a property. And now,

Listen to this news: Brutus and Cassius

Are raising armies. We must act right away.

Let us gather our most trusted friends

And have a meeting. We must decide

What to do about it.

(**They** exit.)

Scene ❷ 🎧

(An army camp in Greece. A drum sounds. **Brutus**, **Lucilius**, **Lucius**, and **soldiers** enter. **Titinius** and **Pindarus** meet them.)

BRUTUS: Lucilius, is Cassius near?

LUCILIUS: Yes, and Pindarus has come to
Deliver greetings from his master, Cassius.

BRUTUS: I accept his greetings.
How did Cassius receive you? Tell me.

LUCILIUS: With courtesy and enough respect—
But not with the same friendliness
He showed me in the past.

BRUTUS: You describe a hot friend cooling.
When love begins to sicken and decay,
It becomes forced ceremony.
There are no tricks in plain and simple faith.
But hollow men are like horses before a race.
They promise spirit and make a brave show,
But during the race, their necks bow down
And, false and worn out, they fail the test.
Is his army coming?

LUCILIUS: They mean to camp nearby tonight.

Some are already here with Cassius.

(**Cassius** and his **soldiers** enter.)

BRUTUS: Listen, he has arrived.

CASSIUS *(to Brutus):* You have done me wrong.

BRUTUS: You gods! Do I wrong my enemies?

And, if not, how can I wrong a brother?

CASSIUS: This show of yours hides wrongs,

And when you do them—

BRUTUS: Cassius, be quiet! Let us not argue

Before the eyes of both our armies.

They should see nothing but love in us.

Tell them to move away.

Then, in my tent, you can speak your anger,

And I will listen to you.

CASSIUS: Pindarus, order our officers

To lead their men a little away from here.

BRUTUS: Lucilius, you do the same.

And let no man come to our tent

Until we have finished our meeting.

Lucius and Titinius will guard the door.

(**All** exit.)

Scene ❸ 🎧 13

(Brutus's tent. **Brutus** and **Cassius** enter, arguing.)

CASSIUS: This is how you have wronged me:
    You have publicly accused Lucius Pella
    Of taking bribes. Because I know him,
    I wrote a letter speaking for his side,
    But you ignored what I said.

BRUTUS: You wronged yourself to write it.

CASSIUS: In such a time as this, it is not right
    To comment on every little offense.

BRUTUS: Let me tell you, Cassius, you yourself
    Are often said to have an itching palm.
    They say that, for gold, you sell honors
    To men who don't deserve them.

CASSIUS: I—an itching palm?
    If you weren't Brutus, by the gods,
    This speech would be your last.

BRUTUS: And if you weren't Cassius,
    You would have been punished by now.

CASSIUS: Punished?

BRUTUS: Remember the Ides of March?
  Didn't great Julius bleed for justice's sake?
  What villain stabbed his body for a reason
  Other than justice? Do we now soil our
  Fingers with bribes and sell our honor?
  I'd rather be a dog, baying at the moon,
  Than be such a Roman.

CASSIUS: Brutus, don't attack me!
  I won't stand for it. I am a soldier,
  Older in experience and more able than you
  To make decisions.

BRUTUS: No, you are not, Cassius.

CASSIUS: I am.

BRUTUS: I say you are not.

CASSIUS: Enough! Think of your health.
  Don't tempt me, or I'll forget myself.

BRUTUS: Away, slight man!

CASSIUS: What are you saying?

BRUTUS: Hear me, for I will speak.
  Must I give way to your rash temper?

CASSIUS: Oh, you gods! Must I go through this?

BRUTUS: This and more. Fret until your proud heart breaks.

Go show your slaves how excited you are,
And make them tremble. Must I bow
Under your angry temper? By the gods,
You'll digest the poison of your anger
Even if it splits you. From this day on,
I'll only laugh at your wasp-like temper.

CASSIUS: Has it come to this?

BRUTUS: You say you are the better soldier.
Prove it, and it shall please me well.
I am always glad to learn of noble men.

CASSIUS: You wrong me every way, Brutus.
I said an older soldier, not a better.
Did I say "better"?

BRUTUS: If you did, I don't care.

CASSIUS: Even Caesar never dared anger me so!

BRUTUS: Enough! You dared not to tempt him.

CASSIUS: Do not presume so much on my love.
I may do something that I shall regret.

BRUTUS: You've already done so.
I feel no terror, Cassius, at your threats.

For I am so strongly armed with honor,
Threats pass by me as the idle wind.
I sent a messenger to you to ask for gold,
And you denied me. I can raise no money
By evil means. I'd rather squeeze money
From my heart and blood than to wring it
From the hard hands of peasants.
You wouldn't help to pay my armies.
Would I have done that to you?
When Marcus Brutus grows so greedy
As to lock away such trash from his friends,
Be ready, gods, with all your thunderbolts,
To dash him to pieces!

CASSIUS: I did not deny you. A fool of a
Messenger brought back the wrong answer.
Brutus has split my heart.
A friend should accept his friend's faults,
But you make mine greater than they are.

BRUTUS: I do not, till you practice them on me.

CASSIUS: You love me not.

BRUTUS: I do not like your faults.

CASSIUS: A friend would not see such faults.

BRUTUS: A flatterer would not—even if
They appeared as huge as a mountain.

CASSIUS: Come, Antony, and young Octavius!
Have your revenge on Cassius alone,
For Cassius is weary of the world!
Hated by one he loves like a brother,
Scolded like a slave, all his faults listed in
A notebook and thrown back in his teeth.
Oh, I could weep my spirit from my eyes!
There is my dagger,
(He offers his dagger to Brutus.)
And here my naked breast, my heart inside.
If you are a Roman, take it out.
I, who denied you gold, will give my heart.
Strike as you did at Caesar. I know that
When you hated him most, you loved him
Better than you ever loved Cassius.

BRUTUS: Put away your dagger. Let it pass.
You carry anger as a flint bears fire—
When struck hard, you show a quick spark,
Then right away you are cold again.

CASSIUS: Has Cassius lived to be no more than
Laughter to his Brutus,
When his bad temper makes him angry?

BRUTUS: When I said such a thing, I was
  bad-tempered, too.

CASSIUS: Do you admit it? Give me your hand.

BRUTUS: And my heart, too.

(They shake hands.)

CASSIUS: Oh, Brutus!

BRUTUS: What's the matter?

CASSIUS: Can't you love me enough to
  Forgive me when the bad temper
  My mother gave me makes me forget?

BRUTUS: I do, Cassius. And from now on,
  When you lose your temper with Brutus,
  He'll think it's your mother scolding him,
    and leave you alone.

POET *(from offstage):* Let me go see them.
  There is some grudge between them.
  It's not good for them to be alone.

LUCILIUS *(from offstage):* You may not.

POET *(from offstage):* Nothing but death will stop
  me.

(A **poet** enters, followed by **Lucilius**, **Titinius**, and **Lucius**.)

CASSIUS: What's going on? What's the matter?

POET: For shame, generals! What's this?
Love and be friends, as you should do.
Listen, for I've seen more years than you.

CASSIUS: Ha, ha! How badly this poet rhymes!

BRUTUS: Get out of here, you bold fellow! Go!

(**Poet** exits.)

BRUTUS: Lucilius and Titinius, tell the officers
To have their men bed down for the night.

CASSIUS: Come yourselves to us immediately, and
bring Messala with you.

(**Lucilius** and **Titinius** exit.)

BRUTUS: Lucius, some wine!

(**Lucius** exits.)

CASSIUS: I did not think you could be so angry.

BRUTUS: Oh, Cassius, I am sick with grief.

CASSIUS: It is not like you to give in to evils
That happen by chance.

BRUTUS: No man bears sorrow better. I must tell you
that Portia is dead.

CASSIUS: What? Portia?

BRUTUS: She is dead.

CASSIUS: How did I escape being killed
When I angered you so? Oh, terrible loss!
Of what sickness did she die?

BRUTUS: She died of missing me—
And grief that Octavius and Mark Antony
Have made themselves so strong.
I heard that before she died,
She fell into a depression. Then when her
Servants left, she swallowed burning coals.

CASSIUS: And she died from that?

BRUTUS: Yes.

CASSIUS: Oh, you immortal gods!

(**Lucius** enters again, with wine and a candle.)

BRUTUS: Speak no more of her. Give me wine.
In this goblet I bury all unkindness, Cassius. *(He drinks.)*

CASSIUS: My heart thirsts for that noble toast!
Fill, Lucius, until the wine overflows the cup.
I cannot drink too much of Brutus's love. *(He drinks.)*

(**Lucius** exits. **Titinius** and **Messala** enter.)

BRUTUS: Come in, Titinius! Messala!
　　Now let's sit close by the candlelight
　　And talk about what we need to do.

(They sit.)

ACT **4**
SCENE
3

　　Messala, I have received letters
　　That young Octavius and Mark Antony
　　March against us with a mighty army.
　　They are heading toward Philippi.

MESSALA: I've had letters saying the same.

BRUTUS: Is there anything else?

MESSALA: Yes. Octavius, Antony, and Lepidus
　　Have had a hundred senators put to death
　　And then seized their property.

BRUTUS: Well, let us start the work that faces
　　Those of us who are still alive.
　　What do you think of marching to Philippi?

CASSIUS: I do not think it wise.

BRUTUS: Your reason?

CASSIUS: It is this:
　　It is better that the enemy seek us.

Let him waste his supplies, tire out his men,
Do himself harm. Meanwhile, we'll lie still
And be rested, quick, alert, and ready.

BRUTUS: Good reasons must give way to better.
The people between here and Philippi
Are on our side only by force.
They begrudge us the supplies we take.
The enemy, marching among them,
Will urge them to join their army.
We can cut them off from this advantage
If we march to Philippi and face them there,
With these people at our back.

CASSIUS: Hear me, good brother—

BRUTUS: Begging your pardon, I'll go on.
You must also note that we've demanded
A great deal from our friends. Our force
Is at full strength. Our cause is ripe.
The enemy grows stronger every day.
We, at full strength, are bound to weaken.
There is a tide in the affairs of men which,
Taken at the flood, leads on to fortune.
If not, the whole voyage of their life

Is wasted in shallow seas and misery.
On such a full sea we are now afloat.
We must take the current while we can—
Or risk losing our chances.

CASSIUS: Then, as you wish, go on.
We'll march and meet them at Philippi.

BRUTUS: The deep of night has crept in as
We talked, and nature demands we sleep.
Let's be stingy with her, and rest a little.
Is there anymore to say?

CASSIUS: No more. Good night.

Early tomorrow we will rise and go.

BRUTUS: Farewell, Messala and Titinius.

Noble Cassius, good night, and rest well.

CASSIUS: Oh, my dear brother!

This night had such a bad beginning.

Let such division never come

Between our souls again, Brutus.

BRUTUS: Everything is well.

CASSIUS: Good night, my lord.

(**All** exit but Brutus, who calls in Lucius and tells him to sleep inside the tent. Lucius falls asleep, and Brutus reads by the light of a candle.)

BRUTUS: How poorly this candle burns!

(The **ghost of Caesar** enters.)

Who comes here?

It must be the weakness of my eyes

That shapes this monstrous apparition.

It advances! Are you anything?

Are you a god, an angel, or a devil that

Makes my blood cold and my hair stand up?

Tell me what you are.

GHOST: Your evil spirit, Brutus.

BRUTUS: Why do you come?

GHOST: To say that you shall see me at Philippi.

BRUTUS: What! I shall see you again?

GHOST: Yes, at Philippi.

BRUTUS: Very well, I will see you at Philippi.

(**Ghost** exits.)

ACT 4
SCENE 3

> Now that I've found courage, you vanish!
> Evil spirit, I would talk more with you.
> Boy! Lucius! Awake!

(Lucius wakes up.)

LUCIUS: My lord?

BRUTUS: Take a message to Cassius. Tell him
> To lead his forces off early in the morning,
> And we will follow him.

LUCIUS: It shall be done, my lord.

(**They** exit.)

ACT 5

Summary

在腓立比的平原，屋大維和安東尼為交戰而準備。喀西約和布魯圖斯聊到抵禦機會渺小時自殺的可能性，布魯圖斯表明他寧願戰死而不願自殺或淪為俘虜。

在戰場的另一方，喀西約和提第尼烏斯討論戰況，喀西約差派提第尼烏斯至戰場另一區去探查該軍是敵還是友。當提第尼烏斯被一群高聲歡呼的騎士包圍時，喀西約以為提第尼烏斯已被俘虜。喀西約認為大勢已失，要求平達路斯殺了他，而平達路斯也聽話照辦。

當提第尼烏斯返回稟告該軍隊為友軍時，他看見喀西約的遺體，並發現喀西約誤解了一切，提第尼烏斯因絕望也自殺。

在戰場另一端，布魯圖斯了解其軍隊正在潰敗，布魯圖斯撲向自己由史特拉托握住的寶劍而亡。安東尼稱布魯圖斯為：「最崇高的羅馬人」，因為他的行為背後有著高貴的動機，而他誓言將給他一場風光的葬禮。

Scene ❶ 🎧

(The plains of Philippi. **Octavius**, **Antony**, and their **troops** enter.)

OCTAVIUS: Now our hopes are answered.
    You said the enemy would not come down,
    But keep to the hills and upper regions.
    It proves not so. Their armies are close.
    They mean to fight us here at Philippi.

ANTONY: Don't worry. I know them well.
    They want us to think they are brave,
    But it is not so.

(A **messenger** enters.)

ACT 5
SCENE 1

MESSENGER: Be ready, generals.
    The enemy comes on gallantly.
    Something must be done at once.

ANTONY: Octavius, lead your troops
    To the left side of the field.

OCTAVIUS: I'll go to the right, you go left.

ANTONY: Why do you cross me now?

OCTAVIUS: I do not cross you, but I will do so.

(Drums sound. **Brutus**, **Cassius**, and their **troops** enter, with **Lucilius**, **Titinius**, and **Messala**.)

BRUTUS: They've stopped. They want to talk.

CASSIUS: Stand fast, Titinius.

OCTAVIUS: Antony, shall we start fighting?

ANTONY: No, we will wait for their attack.

Step forward. The generals want to talk.

(The leaders step toward each other.)

BRUTUS: Words before blows. Is that it, countrymen?

OCTAVIUS: It's not that we love words better—as you do.

BRUTUS: Good words are better than bad strokes, Octavius.

ANTONY: Your bad strokes deliver good words.

I mean the hole you made in Caesar's heart,

Crying "Long live! Hail, Caesar!"

CASSIUS: Your blows' strength is yet unknown.

But as for your words, at Caesar's funeral,

They robbed the bees of their honey.

ANTONY: But not of their sting.

BRUTUS: Oh, yes. You stole their buzzing, too,

And very wisely threaten before you sting.

ANTONY: As you did not, villains, when your
Daggers sliced into the sides of Caesar.
You showed your teeth like apes
And bowed like slaves, kissing Caesar's feet,
While Casca, like a dog,
Struck him in the neck! You flatterers!

CASSIUS *(reminding Brutus that he had wanted to
kill Antony on March 15):* Now, Brutus, you
must blame yourself.
This tongue would not be so offensive today
If Cassius had had his way.

OCTAVIUS: If arguing makes us sweat,
The test of it will turn to redder drops.
Look, I draw a sword against conspirators.
(He draws his sword.) I will not put it away until
Caesar's 33 wounds
Are avenged, or until I die by traitors' swords!

BRUTUS: You cannot die by traitors' hands
Unless you brought them with you!

OCTAVIUS: So I hope.
I was not born to die on Brutus's sword.

JULIUS CAESAR

BRUTUS: If you were the noblest of your family,
You could not die more honorably.

OCTAVIUS: Come, Antony, away!
Traitors, we throw defiance in your teeth.
If you dare fight today, come to the field.
If not, come when you find the courage.

(**Octavius**, **Antony**, and their **troops** exit.)

CASSIUS: The storm is up, and all is at risk.

BRUTUS: Lucilius, listen. A word with you.

(**Lucilius** steps forward, and he and **Brutus** step aside
together, to talk.)

CASSIUS: Messala!

MESSALA *(stepping forward)*: General?

CASSIUS: Messala, this is my birthday.
On this very day Cassius was born.
Give me your hand. Be my witness that,
Against my will, I am forced to risk
All our liberties on this one battle.
You know that I have never believed
In omens. But now I have changed
    my mind.

104

Ravens and crows fly over our heads and
Look down on us as if we were sickly prey.
Their shadows seem like a fatal cover,
Under which our army lies, ready to die.

MESSALA: Do not believe this!

CASSIUS: I only believe it partly,
For my spirit is ready to meet all danger.
(returning to Brutus) Now, noble Brutus,
Since the future is uncertain, let's
Think about the worst that may happen.
If we lose this battle, then this is
The last time we shall speak together.
What are you then determined to do?

ACT 5
SCENE
1

BRUTUS: I always blamed old Cato for the
death he gave himself. I don't know why,
But I find it cowardly to end one's life
Out of fear of what might happen.
Surely it is better to face what might come.

CASSIUS: So, if we lose, you are content to be
Led in triumph through the streets of Rome?

BRUTUS: No, Cassius, no! Do not think that
Brutus will ever go to Rome in chains. Let's
End the work begun on the Ides of March.
I don't know if we shall meet again.
So let us say our last farewell.
Forever and forever, farewell, Cassius!
If we do meet again, why, we shall smile.
If not, then this parting was well-made.

CASSIUS: Forever and forever, farewell, Brutus!
If we do meet again, we'll smile indeed;
If not, it's true this parting was well-made.

(**All** exit.)

Scene ❷

(The field of battle. Trumpets sound. **Brutus** and **Messala** enter.)

BRUTUS: Ride, ride, Messala. Give these orders
   To the forces on the other side. *(He hands
   Messala papers.)*

(Loud trumpets sound.)

   Let them attack at once, for I think
   I see a weakness in Octavius's army.
   Ride, Messala! Let them all come down.

(**All** exit.)

Scene 3 🎧

(Another part of the field. Trumpets sound. **Cassius** and **Titinius** enter.)

CASSIUS: Look, Titinius, watch the villains fly!
   I have turned enemy to my own men.
   This flag-bearer was running away.
   I killed the coward, and took the flag.

TITINIUS: Oh, Cassius, Brutus gave the word
   Too early. He had an advantage,
   But he was too eager. His soldiers took to
   Looting. Now Antony's men surround us.

(**Pindarus** enters.)

PINDARUS: Get away from here, lord, away!
   Mark Antony is in your tents, my lord.

CASSIUS: This hill is far enough. Look, Titinius!
   Are those my tents burning?

TITINIUS: They are, my lord.

CASSIUS: Titinius, quick! Ride over there.
   Find out if those troops are friend or enemy.

TITINIUS: I will return as fast as a thought.

(**Titinius** exits.)

CASSIUS: Pindarus, get higher on that hill.

Watch Titinius. Tell me what you see.

(Pindarus climbs the hill.)

On this day I took my first breath.

Time has come around.

Where I began, and there shall I end.

My life has run its course.

(to Pindarus): Tell me, what news?

PINDARUS *(shouting):* Oh, my lord!

Titinius is surrounded by horsemen

Who are shouting for joy.

It looks as if he's been captured!

CASSIUS: Come down, look no more.

Oh, coward that I am, to live to see,

My best friend taken before my face!

*(**Pindarus** comes down from the hill.)*

Come here, Pindarus. Remember when

I took you prisoner in Parthia? On that day,

I spared your life and made you promise

To do whatever I told you to do. Come now,

Keep your oath. You are now free. With this

Sword that ran through Caesar's belly,

seek my heart. Do not say a word.

Here, take the handle.

When my face is covered,

As it is now, guide the sword.

(**Pindarus** stabs **Cassius**.)

Caesar, you are avenged, even with

The sword that killed you!

(**Cassius** dies.)

PINDARUS: So I am free. Yet I would rather

Not have my freedom in such a way.

Oh, Cassius! I shall run far from here,

Where no Roman shall notice me.

(**Pindarus** exits. **Titinius** and **Messala** enter.)

MESSALA: So far, it's even, Titinius.

Brutus won out over Octavius—

But Cassius's troops were beaten by Antony.

TITINIUS: This news will comfort Cassius.

MESSALA: Where did you leave him?

TITINIUS: On this hill, with his slave Pindarus.

MESSALA: Isn't that he lying on the ground?

TITINIUS: No, this was he, Messala—

But Cassius is no more. Oh, setting sun,

As in your red rays you do sink tonight,
So in his red blood has Cassius's day set.
The sun of Rome is set! Our day is gone.
He must have thought that we had lost.

MESSALA: Oh, what a terrible error!

TITINIUS: Where is Pindarus?

MESSALA: Find him, Titinius, while I go
To meet the noble Brutus. I'll tell him
What happened to Cassius.

TITINIUS: Hurry, Messala. *(Messala exits.)*
Why did you send me forth, Cassius?
Did I not meet your friends?
Didn't you hear their shouts of joy?
You have misunderstood everything!
But, wait, wear this garland on your head.
Brutus told me to give it to you, and I shall.
So come now, Cassius's sword.
Find Titinius's heart. *(He kills himself.)*

*(**Messala** enters with **Brutus**, young **Cato**, and others.)*

BRUTUS: Messala, where is Cassius's body?

MESSALA: Over there. Titinius is mourning it.

BRUTUS: Titinius's face is upward.

CATO: Then he is killed.

BRUTUS: Oh, Caesar, you are still mighty!
Your spirit walks about, and turns
Our swords into our own bodies.

CATO: Brave Titinius!
Look how he has crowned dead Cassius!

BRUTUS: Are any two such Romans like these still
alive?
The last of all the Romans, farewell!
It is impossible that Rome will ever see any
Others like you. Friends, I owe more tears
To this dead man than you shall see me pay.
I shall find time, Cassius, I shall find time.
Come, friends, send his body home
For the funeral. Lucilius, and Cato,
Let us go to the battlefield.
It's three o'clock, and Romans, before night
We shall try our fortune in a second fight.

(**All** exit.)

Scene 4 🎧

(Another part of the field. Trumpets sound. **Soldiers** enter, fighting. Then **Brutus**, young **Cato**, **Lucilius**, and **others** enter.)

BRUTUS: Countrymen, hold up your heads!

CATO: Of course we will!

I will shout my name about the field.

I am Cato, a foe to tyrants!

BRUTUS: And I am Brutus, my country's friend!

(**Brutus** exits. Young **Cato** falls.)

LUCILIUS: Oh, noble Cato, are you down?

Why, you died as bravely as Titinius!

SOLDIER 1 *(to Lucilius)*: Give up, or die!

LUCILIUS: I would rather die than surrender.

Kill me, and you kill Brutus,

And be honored in his death.

SOLDIER 2: Tell Antony that Brutus is our prisoner.

SOLDIER 1: Here comes the general.

(**Antony** enters.)

Brutus is taken! Brutus is taken, my lord!

ANTONY *(looking around)*: Where is he?

ULIUS CAESAR

LUCILIUS: Safe, Antony, he is safe enough.
  I promise you that no enemy shall ever take
  The noble Brutus alive. No, the gods will
  Defend him from so great a shame!

ANTONY *(to Soldier 1)*: This is not Brutus,
  Friend, but I assure you, he is still a prize.
  He was just posing as Brutus to protect him.
  Keep this man safe. Give him all kindness.
  I would rather have such men as friends
  Than enemies. Go on, and see whether
  Brutus is alive or dead. Bring us word
  In Octavius's tent.

(**All** exit.)

Scene ⑤

(Another part of the field. **Brutus** and **Strato** enter.)

BRUTUS: Come, friend. Rest on this rock.

It appears that we cannot win this fight.

The ghost of Caesar appeared to me

Last night. I know my hour has come.

STRATO: Not so, my lord.

BRUTUS: Yes, I am sure that it has.

You see how the battle is going.

Our enemies have beaten us to the pit.

It is better to leap in ourselves

Than to wait until they push us.

Strato, you are a fellow of great respect.

Your life has had some honor in it.

Hold, then, my sword, and turn your face,

While I run upon it. Will you, Strato?

STRATO: Give me your hand first.

Farewell, my lord.

BRUTUS: Farewell, good Strato. *(He runs onto his sword.)*

ACT 5
SCENE 5

Caesar, now be still! I killed you with not half so good a will.

(**Brutus** dies. Trumpets sound. **Octavius**, **Antony**, **Messala**, **Lucilius**, and the **army** enter.)

OCTAVIUS: What man is that?

MESSALA: My master's man. Strato, where is your master?

STRATO: Free from the slavery that binds you, Messala.

The conquerors can only make a fire of him,
For Brutus alone has conquered Brutus.
No other man gains honor by his death.

LUCILIUS: So it should be. I thank you, Brutus,
For proving true what Lucilius said.

OCTAVIUS: I will accept all who served Brutus
Into my service. Fellow, will you join me?

STRATO: Yes, if Messala recommends it.

OCTAVIUS: Do so, good Messala.

MESSALA: How did my master die, Strato?

STRATO: I held the sword, and he ran onto it.

MESSALA: Octavius, take him to follow you.
He did the last service to my master.

ANTONY *(respectfully)*: This was the noblest Roman
of them all.

All the conspirators, except for him,
Did what they did in envy of great Caesar.
Brutus alone acted because he thought
It was for the common good of Rome.
His life was gentle, and the elements
So mixed in him that Nature might stand up
And say to all the world, "This was a man!"

OCTAVIUS: Because of his virtue, let us
Give him all the respect and rites of burial.
His bones shall lie within my tent tonight,
Treated honorably, most like a soldier.
Call the army to rest, and we'll go away,
To share the glories of this happy day.

(**All** exit.)

中文翻譯

簡介 ———————————————————— 英文內文 P. 004

在西元前四十四年的羅馬，身為軍隊將領的朱利厄斯凱撒，在一場激戰中擊敗了名為龐培的羅馬貴族。本劇即由一場公開慶典揭開序幕，但是有幾位支持龐培的貴族因為凱撒愈來愈受擁戴而深感恐懼，他們擔心野心勃勃的凱撒會想當國王——那偉大的羅馬共和國要就此告終了。為了保護他們自己的權力，他們開始密謀除掉他。

出場人物 ———————————————————— P. 005

朱利厄斯凱撒：羅馬政治家與軍隊將領

屋大維：羅馬政客；後來被稱作奧古斯都凱撒，第一任羅馬皇帝

馬克安東尼：羅馬政客、將領和凱撒的好友

雷比達：羅馬政客

馬可斯布魯圖斯、喀西約、喀司加、崔伯尼烏斯、利伽瑞斯、狄西厄斯布魯圖斯、梅泰路斯辛伯與秦納：密謀加害凱撒之人

卡普尼亞：凱撒的妻子

波西亞：布魯圖斯的妻子

西塞羅、波比利烏斯與波比利烏斯雷納：元老院議員們

弗拉維烏斯與馬魯路士：護民官

加圖、盧西留斯、提第尼烏斯、梅薩拉與弗倫尼厄斯：
布魯圖斯的支持者們

阿特米多拉斯：修辭學教師

普布利烏斯：一位年長的紳士

史特拉托與盧修斯：布魯圖斯的僕人們

平達路斯：喀西約的僕人

凱撒的鬼魂

一名占卜者、一名詩人、元老院議員們、市民們、士兵們、平民們、信差們與僕人們

第一幕

●第一場 ————————————————————— P. 007

（在羅馬的一條街道；弗拉維烏斯、馬魯路士與幾名平民上。）

弗拉維烏斯：回家吧，你們這些遊手好閒的傢伙！今天是假日嗎？你們難道不知道沒有正事要辦，在工作日是不能四處走動的嗎？告訴我，你是從事何種行業？

平民一：喔，我是個木匠。

馬魯路士：你的工具何在？何以穿著你最好的衣服？還有你——你是從事何種行業？

平民二：我是補鞋匠，憑著良心在工作，因我是修理磨壞的鞋底。倘若你哪裡壞了，我可以為你修補。

馬魯路士：你這話是何意？嗯，為我修補？你這鹵莽無禮的傢伙。

平民二：怎麼——當然是修補鞋子啊。

弗拉維烏斯：你何以不在店鋪裡？為何領著這些人在街上閒逛？

平民二：為了磨破他們的鞋底，好讓我多點工作做。但是事實上，我們是放了一天假要去見見凱撒，慶祝他凱旋歸來。

馬魯路士：為何慶祝？他是什麼凱旋了？他帶回了什麼俘虜？你們這些木頭、石塊，比毫無知覺的東西更不如！喔，你們這些鐵石心腸，羅馬的殘酷子民！你們不記得龐培了嗎？曾幾何時，你們多次爬上圍牆和高塔，懷中抱著你們的嬰孩，在那兒坐上一整天，耐心等著見到偉大的龐培途經羅馬的街道。等你們看到他的馬車出現之際，難道沒有高聲歡呼到回音憾動堤防底下的台伯河嗎？如今你們卻換上最好的衣服？放一天假偷閒罷工，在他沾染了龐培的鮮血戰勝歸來之時獻花予他？滾吧！速速返家跪地自省！懇求眾神停止瘟疫，不再懲罰你們的忘恩負義。

弗拉維烏斯：去吧，好同胞們──還有，為此過失，集結如你們這般的所有人，帶他們到台伯河畔哭泣，直到河水水位最低處亦親吻最高的河岸。（*所有平民們下。*）瞧瞧他們跑得多快，因心存愧疚而緘默不言。你往那個方向前去朱比特神殿，我則往這個方向。沿途看到任何表揚凱撒的旗幟，一律撤除。

馬魯路士：我們可以這麼做嗎？你明知道這是牧神節的慶典。

弗拉維烏斯：無所謂，莫讓人豎立紀念凱撒勝利的雕像。我來驅走街上的平民們，你見到擁擠的人潮亦如是。我們必須拔除凱撒翅膀上的這些羽毛，免得他振翅高飛到令我們更加害怕的境地。

（*弗拉維烏斯與馬魯路士下。*）

●第二場 —————————————— P. 010

（在公共廣場，號角聲響起；凱撒上，安東尼、卡爾普尼亞、波西亞、狄西厄斯、西塞羅、布魯圖斯、喀西約與喀司加尾隨而上，群眾跟隨在後，人群中有一位占卜者。）

凱撒：卡爾普尼亞！

卡爾普尼亞：在，閣下。

凱撒：在安東尼跑過賽道之時，直接攔住他的去路。安東尼！在跑過卡爾普尼亞的同時，切記要碰觸她。長老們説未生育的婦女，在牧神節的慶典上被參與這神聖賽事之人碰觸，未幾即可懷上孩子。

安東尼：我會記住的。凡是凱撒吩咐要我做的事，我必不負使命。

（號角聲響起。）

占卜者（從人群中）：凱撒！留心三月十五日。

凱撒：此話是何人所言？

布魯圖斯：有位占卜者警告你，要留心三月十五日。

凱撒：讓我看看他的臉。

喀西約：朋友，從人群中出來吧！

凱撒：再説一遍。

占卜者：留心三月十五日。

凱撒：他是癡人説夢，就別理會他了。

（全體下，獨留布魯圖斯與喀西約。）

喀西約：你要去觀賞賽事嗎？

布魯圖斯：我對競賽毫無興趣；我沒有安東尼那般的充沛活力，但是你不必因我而留下，喀西約。我先走一步，你要觀看便去吧。

喀西約：布魯圖斯，我發現你近日似乎有意在躲著我。

布魯圖斯：不，喀西約，我只是最近有些私事煩心，但是不勞我的諸位好友們──包括你在內，喀西約──過度地為我擔憂。我冷落了朋友們，只是因為可憐的布魯圖斯正在內心天人交戰。

喀西約：那就是我誤會了，我始終將此念頭藏在心底。告訴我，好布魯圖斯，你能看到自己的臉嗎？

布魯圖斯：不能，因眼睛除非看到其他東西反射出來的影像，否則是看不見自己的。

喀西約：實在可惜了，布魯圖斯，你沒有鏡子可以照出你藏在心底的價值，讓你自己的眼睛看到。我聽了許多德高望重的羅馬人讚美你，除了名聲不朽的凱撒之外。他們在這亂世中宣洩不滿，祈願高貴的布魯圖斯能有凱撒一般的眼光。

布魯圖斯：你是要引我走向何種危險中，喀西約？你要我在自己身上尋找不屬於我的東西嗎？

喀西約：好布魯圖斯，既然你已知看不見你自己，只能看到鏡中的倒影，那就讓我來當你的鏡子吧，我會讓你看到你自己所不能見之物。

（*舞台後方傳來號角聲和喊叫聲。*）

布魯圖斯：這喊叫聲所指何意？我恐怕人們是在呼喚凱撒膺任他們的國王。

喀西約（*狡詐地*）：喔，你深恐如此嗎？那想必你是不願此事發生了。

布魯圖斯：我是不願──但是我忠愛於他。然而，你何以留住我在此這麼久？你到底想告訴我什麼？倘若不是為了全羅馬的利益，用一隻眼睛看到榮譽，卻用另一隻眼睛看到死亡，那我會對兩者皆冷漠以待。但願眾神為我見證，我對榮譽之名的愛，更甚於我對死亡的恐懼。

喀西約：我深知你有此等美德，一如我熟知你的面容。榮譽是我故事的主題，你和其他人對此生作何想法我不得而知──但是就我而言，我寧死也不願敬畏不如我自身之人。我生來即如凱撒一般自由自在，而你亦如是。你我皆錦衣玉食，也都如他一般能耐受冬日的寒冷。有一回，在一個風大的陰冷之日，凱撒對我說：「喀西約，你是否膽敢與我一同躍入波濤洶湧的台伯河，泳渡而過？」我聽他這麼說，不顧衣著完整就縱身跳進河裡，並邀他一同下水；他也跟著下水了。河中的波濤洶湧，我們懷著英勇的心用盡氣力抵禦湍流，但是尚未游到河流彼岸，凱撒便呼喊：「救我，喀西約，否則我要沉沒了！」於是我從台伯河的波濤中背起了精疲力竭的凱撒。如今此人已被神化──而喀西約只是個卑下的奴才，凱撒無意間點個頭，我就必須在他面前俯首稱臣！他在西班牙的期間染了熱病，發起病來全身顫抖不已！這是真的──這個神也會顫抖！他怯懦的雙唇失了血色，足以震懾世人的眼神也沒了光彩。我聽見他在呻吟；是的，平時舌燦蓮花的他大喊著：「給我來點喝的。」宛如一個生病的姑娘似的。你們眾神啊！我很訝異如此虛弱之人竟能博得全天下的尊敬，一人獨攬所有的榮耀。

（*舞台後方傳來喊叫聲與號角聲。*）

布魯圖斯：群眾又在呼喊了！我相信他們的歡呼，是為了新加
　　　諸在凱撒身上的榮耀。

喀西約：是啊，他像個巨人似地邁開大步走在這狹小的世界
　　　上，而微不足道的我們走在他的巨腿胯下，四處窺視給自
　　　己尋找不名譽的墳墓！人在某些時候得以主宰自己的命
　　　運。親愛的布魯圖斯，性格缺陷並非我們的宿命，而是存
　　　在於我們身上，使我們屈就於他人之下。「布魯圖斯」和
　　　「凱撒」都只是名字，何以凱撒的名字就比你的更受人尊
　　　崇？將這兩個名字寫在一起──你的名字和他的一樣悅
　　　目；念出來──你的也一樣悅耳；秤秤重量──你的也不
　　　比他的輕。如今同時以眾神之名，凱撒吃了什麼肉使他變
　　　得如此偉大？這個時代是蒙羞的！羅馬，你失去了高貴的
　　　血統！自從發生了大洪水之後，有哪個時代只出了一位名
　　　人？當人們談起羅馬之時，何時有人說這寬闊的城牆內只
　　　住了一個人？倘若此地只有一個人，那還稱得上是羅馬嗎？

布魯圖斯：我知道你對我友好，這些事我早已想過，你說的
　　　這番話且容我再行斟酌。此刻我會耐心聽你說；假以時日
　　　我聽到這些崇高的話必會予以回覆，但在此之前，我尊貴
　　　的朋友，請你也仔細思量：如今的布魯圖斯寧可當個平凡
　　　的村民，也不願自稱是羅馬之子。倘若凱撒成了國王，對
　　　羅馬的影響將使我深感惶恐。

喀西約：很高興我這番毫無說服力的話語，能激起布魯圖斯
　　　如此熾烈的熱火。

（凱撒與他的侍從們再上。）

布魯圖斯：賽事已然結束，凱撒回來了。

喀西約：在他們途經此處時，抓住喀司加的衣袖。他必會用
　　　尖酸的口吻，將今日發生的重要大事告知予你。

布魯圖斯：我會的，但是喀西約，你瞧，凱撒的眉宇間透著憤怒的神情，卡爾普尼亞的臉頰蒼白，西塞羅臉上也顯現出他遭到反駁時的生氣模樣。

喀西約：喀司加會告知我們今日發生的事。

凱撒：安東尼！

安東尼：凱撒？

凱撒：將我隨身的侍從們都換成身材圓潤又油頭亮面之人，夜裡得以熟睡。那喀西約看起來清瘦又飢餓，他想太多了，如此之人太過於危險。

安東尼：切莫懼怕他，凱撒，喀西約並不危險，他是個尊貴又備受尊崇的羅馬人。

凱撒：真希望他能吃胖一點！我並不懼怕他──但是我若要懼怕任何人，最應該迴避之人就非那纖瘦的喀西約莫屬。他飽讀詩書、觀察力敏銳，似乎能看穿他人的心思。他和你一樣不喜玩樂，安東尼，也不好音樂。他臉上很少笑容，即使笑了也彷彿是在自嘲，輕蔑地皮笑而肉不笑。此種人見到比自己更偉大者，絕對不會善罷甘休，所以是極其危險之人。我來告訴你要懼怕的是什麼，但我並不懼怕──因我永遠都會是凱撒。站過來我的右側，因我這隻耳朵已聾。現在，把你對他真正的想法告訴我。

（號角聲響起；凱撒與他的侍從們下，獨留喀司加。）

喀司加：你拉住我的斗篷，是有話要對我說嗎？

布魯圖斯：是的，告訴我們今天發生了什麼事令凱撒神情如此哀傷。

喀司加：怎麼，你當時不也在他身邊？

布魯圖斯：倘若我在他身邊，現在就毋需問你了。

喀司加：有人將王冠交予他，他用自己的手背推開了它，然後群眾就開始叫喊。

布魯圖斯：第二次的叫喊所為何事？

喀司加：也是為了同一件事。

喀西約：他們叫喊了三次，最後一次是所為何事？

喀司加：也是為了同一件事。

布魯圖斯：有人將王冠交予他三次嗎？

喀司加：是的，正是如此，他將之推開了三次——每次都比前一次的力道更輕，每次那些暴民也都喊得更大聲。

喀西約：是誰將王冠交予他？

喀司加：正是安東尼。

布魯圖斯：告訴我們來龍去脈，高尚的喀司加。

喀司加：我看到馬克安東尼將王冠交予他——但是那並非真正的王冠，而是小小的冠冕頭飾——誠如我先前所言，他將之推開一次，但是儘管如此，在我看來他其實是很想接受的。接著安東尼又將之交予他，他也再次將之推開，但是在我看來，他的手指是捨不得放開的。然後安東尼又第三次將之交予他，他又再次將之推開；在他拒絕的同時，群眾大聲叫囂，用他們粗糙的雙手鼓掌，繼而拋出他們滿是汗臭味的睡帽，嘴裡吐出熏天的臭氣，因王冠被推開了。那氣味差點嗆得凱撒難以呼吸，只見他突然昏倒在地。至於我，我不敢大笑，因為深恐一開口便會吸入那惡臭之氣。

喀西約：但是，告訴我，凱撒是如何昏倒的？

喀司加：他就倒在市集中，口吐白沫又無法言語。

布魯圖斯：他必定是患了癲癇。

喀西約：不，凱撒並未患有癲癇，倒是你我和誠實的喀司加都患有癲癇。

喀司加：我不知你此話所指何意，我只知道凱撒倒地不起。

布魯圖斯：他甦醒時說了什麼？

喀司加：在他倒地之前，他看到那一群平民因他拒收王冠而歡欣，於是他伸出脖子意欲任其割喉，然後他就倒地不起。等他甦醒之時，他問及他是否做過奇怪的事或說過奇怪的話；他希望眾人以為他是因病而昏倒。他身旁有三、四名婦人大聲呼喊：「多良善的靈魂啊！」然後就衷心地原諒他了。但是毋需理會她們，即使凱撒刺死了她們的母親，她們依然會這麼做！

布魯圖斯：然後他就神情哀傷地離開了？

喀司加：是的。

喀西約：西塞羅有說什麼嗎？

喀司加：有的，他說了希臘語。

喀西約：他說了什麼？

喀司加：那些聽得懂的人彼此相視而笑，然後搖搖頭，但是在我聽來就只是聽不懂的希臘語。我另有其他信息。馬魯路士和弗拉維烏斯扯下讚揚凱撒的旗幟，因而被封了口。就此別過，還發生了更多事，只是我記不清了。

喀西約：你今晚能與我共進晚餐嗎，喀司加？

喀司加：不行，我有事。

喀西約：那你明天能與我共進晚餐嗎？

喀司加：好的——只要我還活著，而你到明天還有這個念頭，而你這頓晚餐也值得一吃。

喀西約：很好，我會恭候大駕。

127

喀司加：明天見。再會了，兩位。

（喀司加下。）

布魯圖斯：喀司加竟然變得如此無禮！他在求學時代可是絕頂聰明啊。

喀西約：至今做起任何大膽或崇高的事，他仍是絕頂聰明。此般無禮乃是他機敏才智的調味劑，能讓人有更好的胃口去消化他所說的話。

布魯圖斯：你說是就是吧。我也就此告退，明天你若有事與我相談，我就到你府上見你；或者，只要你願意，我也可以在寒舍恭候你的大駕。

喀西約：好的。在此之前，心繫這天下吧。（**布魯圖斯下。**）布魯圖斯，你很是尊貴，但是我發現你可能會心志動搖而失了榮耀，所以尊貴的人還是和尊貴的人往來相處才是，因誰人能意志堅定到不會被誘惑？凱撒待我嚴苛──但是他與布魯圖斯的感情篤厚。倘若我是布魯圖斯，而他是喀西約，他打動不了我的。今晚我會寫一些字條從他的窗戶扔進去，偽裝成是好幾位市民所寫的。這些字條會表達羅馬對他名聲的高度評價，然後簡短提及凱撒的野心。在此之後，就讓凱撒自己當心吧，因我們要撼動他的心志，否則未來的日子只會更難過。

（喀西約下。）

● 第三場————————————————————————P. 025

（在羅馬的一條街道，雷聲隆隆，閃電掠過天際。喀司加從一側上，劍已出鞘，西塞羅從另一側上。）

西塞羅：你好，喀司加，你是否已護送凱撒返家？你為何上氣不接下氣，又何以用那種眼神盯著我看？

喀司加：喔，西塞羅，我見過暴風雨中的狂風折斷橡樹，也見過海上捲起高聳入雲霄的翻天巨浪，但是我直到今晚的此時此刻，才看到有火焰落下的風暴！若非是天庭有戰爭肆虐，就是世人激怒了眾神，而眾神意欲毀滅世界。

西塞羅：哎呀，你看到了什麼？

喀司加：一名平民奴隸——你也認識他——伸出了他的左手，手上燃著二十把火炬加起來那般的烈焰，但是他的手並未燒灼！除此之外——我後來便未曾收起我的劍——我在朱比特神殿附近遇見一隻獅子在遊蕩，牠盯著我看，與我擦肩而過！我看到上百個面色死白的女人，信誓旦旦地宣稱自己看到著火的男人在街上走來走去！昨天正午，屬於黑夜的貓頭鷹坐在市集上尖聲鳴叫。發生了諸如此類的事，切莫再說：「事出必有因，這些事再自然也不過。」因我相信那是關於未來的厄兆。

西塞羅：是啊，現下確實怪事特別多，但是這些徵兆或許不是你想的那個意思。凱撒明天會前往朱比特神殿嗎？

喀司加：會的，因他囑託安東尼帶口信給你。

西塞羅：那就晚安了，喀司加。這個動亂的夜晚不適合散步。

喀司加：再會了，西塞羅。

（西塞羅下；喀西約上。）

喀西約：來者何人？

喀司加：羅馬人。

喀西約：喀司加，聽聲音就知道了。

喀司加：你的耳朵很靈。好個夜晚！

喀西約：喀司加，我可以說出一個最像這可怕夜晚的人，他打雷、閃電、敞開墳墓、宛如今天在朱比特神殿的那頭獅子似地吼叫。此人在個人的行為上不比你或我更偉大，但是他如同這些奇怪的徵兆一樣令人畏懼又強大。

喀司加：你指的是凱撒吧，喀西約？

喀西約：不論是誰都無所謂，因今日的羅馬人亦如他們的祖先一般是血肉之軀。但是我們好可悲啊！我們父親的心志已死，而我們受到母親靈魂的制約，我們的行為讓自己顯得柔弱有如女子。

喀司加：他們確實說元老院的議員們明天有意擁立凱撒為王；他將戴上王冠統領海陸二界，除了義大利本地之外的各個角落。

喀西約：那我知道我該將這把匕首用於何處了。（*他用他的匕首指向自己的胸口。*）喀西約將使喀西約重獲自由。眾神啊，以此使弱者變成最強壯；眾神啊，以此使所有暴君都被推翻。沒有石造的高塔、鍛造黃銅的牆壁、密不通風的地牢、堅韌的鐵鍊能關得住堅強的心志。厭倦了這俗世枷鎖的生命，從未曾欠缺自我了斷的力量。倘若我知道會如此，就讓全世界都知道吧！這我所承受的暴政，隨時可依我的意願而結束它。

（*雷聲大作。*）

喀司加：我亦如是。所以每個奴隸都有能力，親手結束自己被俘虜的日子。

喀西約：凱撒何以會是個暴君？可憐的人啊！我知道他不會
是狼，只不過他視羅馬人為羔羊。你用脆弱的稻草生起大
火，當羅馬成了點燃凱撒的卑劣野心之火的燃料時，羅馬
豈不成了無用的垃圾？然而，喔，悲傷，你引領我去了何
處？或許我正在心甘情願的奴隸面前如是說，倘若如此，
我知道我的言行必受報應，但是我身懷武器，危險嚇唬不
了我。

喀司加：你說話的對象是喀司加，我可不是露齒而笑的告密
者，我認同你的說法。（*他們握手。*）你要堅定意志，我會大
步邁出我這隻腳，跨出最大的步伐。

喀西約：現已談成了一筆好交易。聽著，喀司加，我已然說
服幾位最德高望重的羅馬人，協助我做一件可敬而危險之
事；他們正在等著我。我們計畫要做的事，宛如這個駭人
的夜晚——最血腥、火爆又可怕。

（*秦納上。*）

喀司加：站過來一點，有個步履匆忙的人來了。

喀西約：是秦納，我從他走路的姿態就認得出來；他是我們
的朋友。秦納，你要往何處去？

秦納：我正要去找你。他是何人？

喀西約：他是喀司加，與我們同一陣營。

秦納：那就太好了。好可怕的一個夜晚！我們有兩、三個人看到了奇怪的景象。

喀西約：其他人都在等著我嗎？

秦納：是的。喔，喀西約，倘若你能說服尊貴的布魯圖斯加入我們的陣營——

喀西約：切莫擔憂，好秦納，將這張紙條放在布魯圖斯能看到之處，把這另一張紙擲入他的窗戶，再將這最後一張塗了蠟，放在他的祖先老布魯圖斯的雕像上頭。等你完成了這幾件事，再去老地方與我們會合。其他人都已經到那兒了嗎？

秦納：除了梅泰路斯辛伯以外的人都到了，他去你的住處找你。我這就去將這幾張紙，照你的吩咐處理好。

（秦納下。）

喀西約：來吧，喀司加，你我在天亮之前一同前去布魯圖斯的住處找他。他十之八九已經投入我們的陣營——下次我們再見面之時，他將全心全意與我們並肩作戰。

喀司加：喔，他在人們心中的地位崇高！在我們身上看似邪惡的特質，一旦有了布魯圖斯的加入，都將成為高尚的美德。

喀西約：你對他的價值瞭若指掌，也深知我們有多麼需要他。我們出發吧，因此刻已過了午夜，我們將在黎明破曉時喚醒他，說服他加入我們的陣營。

（喀西約與喀司加下。）

第二幕

● 第一場 —————————————————— P. 033

（布魯圖斯上，與盧修斯一同走進他的花園。）

布魯圖斯：送一支蠟燭到我的書房，盧修斯，點燃之後再來告知我。

盧修斯：好的，主人。

（盧修斯下。）

布魯圖斯（竊語）：如何才是對羅馬最好的？想必是要凱撒死。於我而言，我個人並無除掉他的理由，但是為了全民的福祉又何如？他想要膺任為王，問題是這又能如何改變他的本質。晴朗的白晝會有蛇出來活動，走路時要小心為上。賦予王冠等於加諸毒刺予

他，隨他意志可能會變得危險。在區別懊悔和權力之時，偉大的高貴身分會被人濫用。我未曾見過凱撒的情感戰勝他的理智，但眾所周知謙卑是野心方興未艾時的梯子；爬上梯子的人會抬頭看，但是等他爬上最高的一階，他就會在梯子上仰望天空，輕蔑他方才爬過的底下幾階。凱撒也有可能這樣；倘若他真的如此，我們就必須防患於未然，因此我們要視他為蛇卵，待孵化之後就會變得致命，必須在他孵化之前就除之而後快。

（盧修斯再上。）

133

盧修斯：蠟燭已經點燃，主人，但是在你的書房中，我找到這張紙；它原本不在那兒。

（盧修斯將信件交予布魯圖斯。）

布魯圖斯：明天不就是三月十五日嗎？

盧修斯：我不知道，主人。

布魯圖斯：去看看日曆再來告知予我。

（盧修斯下。）

布魯圖斯：流星劃過天際，給我足夠的光線方便閱讀。（他拆開信件閱讀。）「布魯圖斯，你正在酣睡，快點醒來看看你自己！說話、攻擊、救救羅馬！布魯圖斯，你仍在酣睡，快醒來！」經常有人將諸如此類的字條從我書房的窗戶投進來，這是要我說話和攻擊嗎？喔，羅馬，我承諾必定會拯救你！

（盧修斯再上。）

盧修斯：主人，明天正是三月十五日。

（從舞台後方傳來敲門聲。）

布魯圖斯：很好，快去應門吧。
（盧修斯下。）自喀西約初次提及凱撒的不是之後，我便夜不成眠。想到了可怕的事，又尚未能採取行動，等待的時間如惡夢一般煎熬。我的內心在天人交戰，而人的心境宛若一個小王國遭逢叛亂似的狀態。

（盧修斯再上。）

盧修斯：喀西約帶了一些人來訪。

布魯圖斯：其他的人你認識嗎？

盧修斯：他們皆以斗篷藏起面容。

布魯圖斯：讓他們進來。(盧修斯下。) 他們是密謀者。喔，陰謀！難道在邪惡最是自由的夜裡，你還是羞於露出你的面容嗎？那麼到了白晝，你又如何找得到足以藏起你羞恥面容的漆黑洞穴？莫要再找了，陰謀，就藏在笑容和友善的表情之中吧。

(喀西約、喀司加、狄西厄斯、秦納、梅泰路斯辛伯與崔伯尼烏斯等陰謀者上。)

喀西約：日安，布魯圖斯，我們是否吵醒了你？

布魯圖斯：我早已起床，其實是徹夜未眠。與你一同來訪的這幾位我都認識嗎？

喀西約：是的，你全都認識——在場的每一位也都崇敬你。我們都希望你對自己的看法，也能和每位尊貴的羅馬人對你的看法一樣。

布魯圖斯：歡迎他們諸位到訪寒舍。請逐一地把手給我吧。

喀西約：那就讓我們宣誓我們的決心。

布魯圖斯：不，切莫發誓，我們需要的僅是充分的理由，此外又何需其他的動力？羅馬人的承諾就足以凝聚眾人了；我們此舉是不成功便成仁。祭司、懦夫和習於被傷害的受苦之人才需要誓言，切莫一心想著我們需要誓言而玷污我們崇高的理由，抑或是損及我們精神的力量。倘若我們當中有人違背承諾，羅馬人所流的每一滴鮮血都要蒙受污名。

喀西約：那西塞羅呢？我們要問他嗎？

喀司加：不能將他排拒在外。

梅泰路斯：是啊，讓他加入吧！他的滿頭白髮必能為我們博得好感；人們會說是他的判斷左右我們的行動，我們的年少輕狂之於他的德高望重必是相形見絀。

布魯圖斯：切莫讓他加入，因他決不會參與他人起頭的行動。

喀西約：那就將他除名吧。

狄西厄斯：除凱撒之外不傷任何人嗎？

喀西約：問得好，狄西厄斯。我認為備受凱撒青睞的馬克安東尼，亦不應於凱撒死後獨留於世。他精明狡黠，日後可能會危害到我們；為免養虎為患，就讓安東尼陪著凱撒一起殞命吧。

布魯圖斯：砍去頭顱再割除四肢，似乎太嫌血腥殘忍了些，因安東尼不過只是凱撒的左膀右臂。就讓我們當獻祭者即可，莫為屠夫。我們要群起反抗凱撒的狼子野心，而在人的心靈上是不需要流血的。真希望我們能擊潰凱撒的野心，卻不傷及他的人，只是很無奈，凱撒必須以鮮血償債！我高貴的朋友們，讓我們放膽去殺了他，但是莫因憤怒而衝動行事，要將他雕琢成獻祭給眾神的佳餚，而非隨意切

割成餵狗的肉塊，如此才顯出我們所為之必要，而非出於妒忌而痛下殺手。讓全民百姓都用此般眼光看待我們，稱我們為清理門戶，而非殺人兇手。至於馬克安東尼——切莫多想，等到凱撒的頭顱被割下，他這條臂膀也不成氣候了。

喀西約：但是他仍可能構成威脅，因他始終忠於凱撒——

布魯圖斯：好喀西約，切莫懼怕他。倘若他忠於凱撒，他也只能自盡以示追隨，因

過度悲傷而死，但是我不認為他會這麼做，畢竟他非常熱愛運動競賽和交際應酬。

崔伯尼烏斯：沒有理由懼怕安東尼，讓他活著吧，因他日後會對此事一笑置之。

（時鐘響起。）

布魯圖斯：該是道別的時候了。

喀西約：凱撒今天會不會出門，我們仍不得而知。他近來非常迷信，今晚不尋常的恐怖詭譎，再加上占卜者的預警，他今天可能不會走近朱比特神殿。

狄西厄斯：毋需擔憂，我可以說服他前往。他喜歡聽橫衝直撞的獨角獸被樹木愚弄、熊被鏡子愚弄、獅子被網子愚弄，以及人被諂媚奉承者愚弄的故事，但是當我提及他憎惡諂媚奉承者之時，他說確實如此──內心卻是無比歡喜。讓我去試試看，因我知道該如何與他對話，我會說服他前去朱比特神殿。

喀西約：我們會一同前去攔下他。

布魯圖斯：是八點鐘，時間沒錯吧？

秦納：最晚八點鐘要到，莫要遲到。

梅泰路斯：利伽瑞斯不喜歡凱撒，因他為龐培說情而遭受凱撒盛怒以待；不知你們為何沒人想過找他一起加入。

布魯圖斯：去找他，好梅泰路斯，我也可以請他來助我們一臂之力。

喀西約：天色將明，布魯圖斯，我們也該告辭了，各位莫忘今日所言，要證明你們是真正的羅馬人。

布魯圖斯：諸位，作出神清氣爽的喜悅神情！莫讓人從我們臉上看出不軌意圖，我們必須像演員似地佯裝，所以，各位早安了。(**全體下，獨留布魯圖斯。**)孩子！盧修斯！熟睡了？無妨，好好享受甜美安穩的睡眠吧。你是如此地無憂無慮，難怪你能酣睡如是。

(**波西亞上。**)

波西亞：布魯圖斯，我的夫君！

布魯圖斯：波西亞，你何以如此早起？

波西亞：我在擔心你啊，布魯圖斯，你最近有點不似尋常，請告訴我你為何事煩心。

布魯圖斯：我只是身體微恙罷了。

波西亞：怎麼——布魯圖斯病了嗎？但是他仍偷偷溜出溫暖的被窩，冒著病情可能加重的風險在夜裡外出？不，我的布魯圖斯，你想必是有心事，而我有權知其詳。算我跪下來求你了，看在我們的愛情份上，告訴我究竟所為何事。昨晚是何人前來訪你？我知道他們一行有六、七個人，即便天色昏暗卻仍蒙面。

布魯圖斯：切莫下跪，我的好波西亞。

波西亞：倘若你一如往常，我就毋需下跪了，高貴的布魯圖斯。

(**從舞台後方傳來敲門聲。**)

布魯圖斯：有人敲門，你先進屋裡去吧，我稍後再將我內心的秘密告訴你。

(**波西亞下；盧修斯上，領著利伽瑞斯。**)

布魯圖斯：凱厄斯利伽瑞斯，你好嗎？(**對盧修斯：**)孩子，你先迴避。

（盧修斯下。）

利伽瑞斯：我知曉你心中盤算著一項以榮譽為名的高尚計畫。

布魯圖斯：確實如此，利伽瑞斯。

利伽瑞斯：羅馬的靈魂！高貴父母所生的英勇兒子！你讓我不快樂的精神重新復甦。我們要做什麼？

布魯圖斯：能讓有病之人重新完整的大事。

利伽瑞斯：難道沒有一些完整之人應該被迫病倒嗎？

布魯圖斯：我們要確保結果是如此。至於詳情如何，我的凱厄斯，待我們在前往下手地點的途中我再告訴你。

利伽瑞斯：帶路吧，我全心全意地追隨你──去做我目前毫不知情的事。只要有布魯圖斯領我前進就足矣。

布魯圖斯：那就跟隨我吧。

（布魯圖斯與利伽瑞斯下。）

（在凱撒的住家；雷電交加；凱撒上，身穿他的睡袍。）

凱撒：今晚無論天地皆不平靜，卡爾普尼亞三度在睡夢中驚聲呼喊：「救命啊！他們謀殺了凱撒！」──來者何人？

（一名僕人上。）

僕人：主人有何吩咐？

凱撒：請祭司安排獻祭，事成之後再把他們的意見告訴我。

僕人：我會的，主人。

（僕人下；卡爾普尼亞上。）

卡爾普尼亞：你這是做什麼，凱撒？你有事要外出嗎？你今天不宜出門！

凱撒：凱撒是要出門，威脅我之人只盯著我背影瞧，他們看到我的臉就會消失無蹤。

卡爾普尼亞：我從不相信預兆，唯如今我因之而心生恐懼。有人言道有隻母獅在羅馬街頭生產；昨晚墳墓大開，放出了亡靈；暴躁的戰士們在雲端群起列隊激戰；鮮血滴落在朱比特神殿，空氣中充滿戰鬥聲、馬的嘶鳴聲和垂死之人的呻吟聲，還有鬼魂在街頭慘叫。喔，凱撒！這些事都頗為蹊蹺，令我恐懼不已。

凱撒：無所不能的眾神早已安排好的事，還能如何避免之？然而凱撒非去不可，因這些預兆可能與任何人相關，其所指未必為凱撒。

卡爾普尼亞：當乞丐死時，沒人會見到彗星。天上繁星只因列王之死而閃耀。

凱撒：懦夫在死前就已死了許多次，然而英勇之人卻只會嘗到一次死亡的滋味。在我至今聽聞的許多奇事之中，似乎最詭異的是人對死亡的恐懼。既然死亡是必然的結局，將死之時誰也躲不過。（僕人再上。）祭司們怎麼說？

僕人： 他們說你今日不宜外出。他們殺了牲畜獻祭，卻怎麼也找不到心臟！

凱撒： 眾神是為了羞辱怯懦之舉才這麼做。倘若凱撒因恐懼而留在家中，那他就是無心的牲畜。不，凱撒不應如此，危險當知凱撒比它更危險！我們有如同一胎的兩頭獅子，但是我比它年長又更令人生畏，所以凱撒應當出門。

卡爾普尼亞： 哎呀，我的夫君！你的智慧被你的自信給吞噬了。今日切莫外出，就當是因為我的恐懼而非你的害怕而留在家中！我們且派馬克安東尼前往元老院，他會說你今日身體不適。就讓我跪地懇求，此事請依我所願。（她跪下。）

凱撒： 就讓馬克安東尼說我身體不適吧。為了滿足你所願，我暫且留在家中。（凱撒扶卡爾普尼亞起身。）（狄西厄斯上。）狄西厄斯布魯圖斯來了，就讓他代為轉達吧。

狄西厄斯： 早安，尊貴的凱撒！我前來陪你一同前往元老院。

凱撒： 你正好趕得及代我問候元老院議員們，通知他們我今日無法前去。說「無法」是虛假，說「我不敢」更虛假。我今天就不去了，代我轉告他們，狄西厄斯。

卡爾普尼亞： 就說他身體抱恙。

凱撒： 難道要凱撒說謊嗎？我長年征戰沙場，竟不敢將實情告訴那些老人？狄西厄斯，就告訴他們凱撒不會前去。

狄西厄斯： 最高尚的凱撒，告訴我原因何在——免得我轉達了你的話卻成為別人的笑柄。

凱撒： 此乃我的意願，我不去；元老院聽聞此言即已足矣。不過，我就私下告訴你原因吧，是卡爾普尼亞要我留在家中，她昨晚夢見她看到我的雕像，彷彿有上百個噴水孔的噴泉似地湧出鮮血，許多欣喜的羅馬人笑著前來洗手。她視之為警訊與邪兆的預告，於是她跪地懇求我今日留在家中。

狄西厄斯：但此夢境是另有所指！此乃美好又幸福的景象，你的雕像從許多噴水管湧出鮮血，許多羅馬人笑著前來洗手，意謂著你的鮮血將振興羅馬，很多偉大的人將前來請求你的賜福與認同；這才是卡爾普尼亞夢境的真義。

凱撒：你説得真是太好了。

狄西厄斯：我還有話要説，元老院決議在今日加冕偉大的凱撒為王；倘若你説你不去，他們可能會改變心意，況且你這似乎是用嘲弄的語氣在説：「元老院可以改日再加冕──等凱撒的妻子作了好夢再説。」倘若凱撒躲在家中，莫不會有耳語揣測「凱撒是在害怕」？凱撒，請原諒我如是忖度，但我是出於對你的景仰才這麼做。

凱撒：如今看來你的恐懼實為愚蠢不堪，卡爾普尼亞！我為聽信你所言而感到羞恥。去取我的長袍來，我必須出門了。（普布利烏斯、布魯圖斯、利伽瑞斯、梅泰路斯、喀司加、崔伯尼烏斯與秦納上。）普布利烏斯也來隨同我前往了。

普布利烏斯：早安，凱撒。

凱撒：歡迎你，普布利烏斯。怎麼你也如此早起，布魯圖斯？早安，喀司加與諸位，是何時辰了？

布魯圖斯：凱撒，時辰已過八點鐘。

凱撒：感謝諸位前來探訪我。（安東尼上。）瞧，就連昨晚深夜方歸的安東尼也起床了。早安，安東尼。

安東尼：早安，最尊貴的凱撒。

凱撒：（對一名僕人）進屋去，請他們準備一些茶點。好了，秦

布魯圖斯：你看，他走向凱撒了。看緊他。

喀西約：布魯圖斯，我們該如何是好？

布魯圖斯：喀西約，你先冷靜。波比利烏斯不會將我們的計畫告訴凱撒；他在微笑，凱撒並未面有異色。

喀西約：崔伯尼烏斯已準備就緒。你看──他已引開馬克安東尼。

（安東尼與崔伯尼烏斯下。）

狄西厄斯：梅泰路斯辛伯何在？他該向凱撒提出請求了。

秦納：喀司加，你必須先舉起你的手。

（他們走進元老院。）

凱撒：眾人皆已準備就緒？凱撒及其元老院有何事待議？

梅泰路斯（跪地）：最偉大的凱撒，梅泰路斯辛伯將他的心袒露在你面前。

凱撒：我必須阻止你，辛伯。此般行禮可能驅使平凡人修改法律，但是我不為所動。你的兄弟被驅逐出境是有原因的，倘若你行此大禮是為了代他求情，那我必定當你是條狗似地一腳踹開。凱撒不會做出不公正之事，也不會毫無原因就改變心意。

梅泰路斯：難道沒有任何人比我更應該為我被驅逐的兄弟求情嗎？

布魯圖斯（跪地）：我親吻你的手──但不是出於奉承，凱撒。請求你准許普布利烏斯辛伯返家。

凱撒：什麼，布魯圖斯？

喀西約（跪地）：請赦免，凱撒！凱撒，請赦免！我伏於你的腳邊，懇求你赦免普布利烏斯辛伯的罪。

凱撒：倘若我像你們一樣，我會為之所動。倘若我也去央求他人，或許苦苦哀求能夠感動我，但是我如北極星一般恆常不變，與夜空中的其他星辰不同。夜空中有繁星點綴，每一顆無不閃爍發亮，但是只有一顆永遠在原地不動。人世間也是一樣，充滿了人；人是血肉之軀，有憂有慮。然而在所有的人當中，我知道只有一個人的姿態是屹立不搖，他是八風吹不動；那人就是我。即使是此事，也讓我表態吧。我堅持將普布利烏斯辛伯驅逐出境，也堅持不改變心意。

秦納（跪地）：喔，凱撒──

凱撒：走開！難道你們自以為能抬起奧林帕斯山嗎？

狄西厄斯（跪地）：偉大的凱撒──

喀司加：雙手，代我發言吧！

（喀司加行刺凱撒，其他人亦起身持刀刺向凱撒，布魯圖斯最後行動。）

凱撒：你也是嗎，布魯圖斯？那就倒地吧，凱撒！

（凱撒死去。）

秦納：解放！自由！暴政已死！
　　快去宣布消息！在街上大
　　喊！

布魯圖斯：各位人民和議員
　　們，切莫恐慌，不要逃跑，
　　冷靜以待，野心已付出代價。

喀司加：前往講壇，布魯圖斯。

狄西厄斯：喀西約也去。

布魯圖斯：普布利烏斯何在？

秦納：在此，因這一切而困惑
　　不已。

梅泰路斯：大家挨緊一點，準備應戰，以防萬一有凱撒的一
　　些餘黨可能會──

布魯圖斯：切莫論及戰鬥。普布利烏斯，莫要擔心，我們不會傷害你或其他羅馬人。

喀西約：去告訴他們，普布利烏斯，小心別被衝向我們的人民傷了你。

布魯圖斯：可憐又困惑的普布利烏斯！讓我們這些行刺的人自行付出代價吧，莫要傷及無辜。

（崔伯尼烏斯再上。）

喀西約：安東尼何在？

崔伯尼烏斯：在震驚之餘逃回家了。男女老少皆瞠目結舌，然後驚慌哭喊，彷彿世界末日似地四下逃竄。

布魯圖斯：命運啊，我們未幾即可知曉你意欲如何！我們知道自己早晚會死，只是不確定自己何時會死。

喀西約：哎呀，減少二十年的壽命，就少了許多年恐懼死亡的日子。

布魯圖斯：既然如此，那我們就是凱撒的朋友，減少了他恐懼死亡的時日。俯下身來，羅馬人，讓我們用凱撒的鮮血洗手吧，洗到手肘，塗在我們的劍上，然後再一起走出去，走上市集，將我們染血的武器高舉到頭頂上，一齊大喊：「和平、自由與解放！」

喀西約：那就俯下身來洗滌吧！（他們用凱撒的鮮血沾染雙手與劍。）未來還有多少年，在尚未誕生的國家、操著尚未有人知曉的口音，會重演我們這偉大的一幕！此情此景有多常上演，就多常有人稱我們是國家的解放者。

狄西厄斯：現在怎麼辦？我們要走了嗎？

喀西約：是的，無一例外。讓布魯圖斯帶頭，我們尾隨在後——羅馬最大膽和最良善的心。

（安東尼的僕人上。）

布魯圖斯：且慢，來者何人？是安東尼的朋友？

僕人（跪地）：正是如此，布魯圖斯，我的主人要我下跪，他還交代我要這麼說：布魯圖斯是尊貴、睿智、勇敢而誠實，凱撒是偉大、果敢、忠誠又博愛世人，說我景仰布魯圖斯和崇敬他，說我懼怕、崇敬和愛戴凱撒。倘若布魯圖斯能讓安東尼平安地前去面見他，聽聽凱撒理應被殺死的原因，那麼他會向布魯圖斯展現應有的尊崇，對還活在世上的他比對死去的凱撒更加敬愛。他會懷著真心實意，追隨冠上新頭銜的布魯圖斯。此乃我家主人安東尼所言。

布魯圖斯：你的主人既睿智又英勇，不負我對他的期望。倘若他願意，就請他前來相談。我會應允他的要求——而且以我的名譽起誓，我會讓他毫髮無傷地離開。

僕人：我這就去轉告他。

（僕人下。）

布魯圖斯：我知道他會是朋友。

喀西約：但願如此，唯我內心仍然懼怕他。

（安東尼再上。）

布魯圖斯：他來了。歡迎你，馬克安東尼。

安東尼（看到遺體）：喔，偉大的凱撒！你竟橫死於此？你所有的凱旋、榮耀、勝利，都縮在這小小的一方土地了嗎？再會了！各位，我不知你們意欲如何，還有誰必須死？倘若是我，那就沒有比凱撒之死更好的時機，也沒有比你的劍更合適的武器，畢竟它沾染了全天下最尊貴的鮮血。我懇求你，倘若你視我為你的敵人，現在就如你所願吧，趁著你染血的雙手還冒煙發著腥臭。若我能有上千年的壽命，也找不到更好的時間地點可以赴死了，就讓我陪著凱撒被你殺死橫屍於此，因你是當前最高的精神指標。

布魯圖斯：安東尼，莫再懇求我們殺死你！我知道我們看似血腥又殘忍，你看見我們的雙手和這個（**指著凱撒的遺體**。）：它們做出的濺血之事。你沒看到我們充滿遺憾的心，但以火滅火卻使火勢更大，以遺憾安撫遺憾亦更加深了遺憾。我們因遺憾羅馬所承受的苦難，而對凱撒做出了此等暴行，但是於你而言，馬克安東尼，我們的劍尖已鈍，我們的懷抱和內心皆懷著愛與尊敬來接納你。

喀西約：你和任何人一樣擁有發言權，決定我們的新領導人。

布魯圖斯：暫且耐心等候，等我們安撫好此時充滿恐懼的人心，我會告訴你為何如此敬愛凱撒的我，會對他做出如此大逆不道之事。

安東尼：我對你的智慧毫無疑慮，但請每個人伸出他染血的手，與我握手表示友善。（**他們都握了手**。）諸位，我能說什麼？你們必定視我為叛逆者——若非懦夫就是阿諛奉承之人。我確實敬愛你，凱撒，喔，這是真的！倘若你的靈魂正在俯瞰著我們，看到你的安東尼正在你未寒的屍骨前，握住你敵人染血的手與之言和，你想必是比死了更悲痛。倘若我有如你的傷口那般多的眼睛，淚水如你的鮮血湧出地那般快，那敢情好過我在此與你的敵人友好往來。原諒我，朱利厄斯！你被圍困在此，勇敢的鹿！你倒在這兒，獵人們身染你的鮮血站在此地。喔，世界啊，你是這頭鹿的森林。喔，世界啊，這其實是你的心。你躺臥於此，彷彿被許多王子們殺死的一頭鹿！

喀西約：馬克安東尼，我不怪你讚美凱撒，但是此言何意？我們還能視你為朋友嗎？

安東尼：所以我才與你們握手。我只是低頭看著凱撒，一時動搖了心志。我敬愛你們諸位，願意與你們為友——但願你們能告訴我何以認定凱撒是危險人物。

布魯圖斯：我們有名正言順的理由，安東尼，即便你是凱撒之子，你也會覺得心服口服。

安東尼：這是我唯一的要求。此外，請應允我將他的遺體移往市集，讓我以朋友的身分在他的葬禮上發言。

布魯圖斯：我應允你的所求，馬克安東尼。

喀西約：布魯圖斯，借一步說話。（*向布魯圖斯竊語：*）此事宜三思而後行。倘若安東尼在他的葬禮上發言，你知道他的所言能有多感動人心嗎？

布魯圖斯（*向喀西約竊語*）：我會先行發言，告訴他們為何凱撒必須死，讓他們知道安東尼是在我們的應允之下發言，我們也意欲給予凱撒死者應有的所有榮譽。此舉對我們是利多於弊。

喀西約：我仍然覺得此舉不妥。

布魯圖斯：馬克安東尼，移走凱撒的遺體吧。你不能在發言中怪罪我們，但是你可以盡情讚揚凱撒的好。就說你的發言乃經我們所應允──否則你將不得出席他的葬禮。你將在我發言的同一講壇發表言論，並且是在我說完之後。

安東尼：我也正有此意。

布魯圖斯：那就帶著遺體隨我們同往吧。

（*全體下，獨留安東尼。*）

安東尼：喔，原諒我，你這染血的一坏土，原諒我順服於殺死你的這群兇手！你是活在時代潮流中最尊貴之人的殘骸。願災難降臨淌流這尊貴

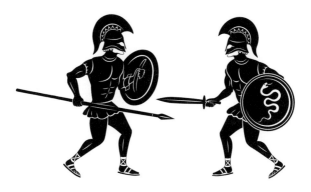

鮮血的那隻手！但願那些人的四肢皆受詛咒。暴烈的內戰將撼動義大利，隨處可見血腥與殘酷之事，致使母親們看到孩子因戰爭而被碎屍萬段時也只能微笑以對。凱撒急欲復仇的靈魂，將以國王的聲音高喊「浩劫！」，讓戰爭的足跡悄悄溜走。此一惡行將在土地之上發臭，而腐爛的屍體則央求著被掩埋。（*屋大維的僕人上。*）你是屋大維凱撒的僕人，對吧？

僕人：是的，馬克安東尼。

安東尼：凱撒要他前來羅馬。

僕人：屋大維閣下收到凱撒的來信，正在趕往此地的途中。他差遣我來告訴你——（*他看到遺體。*）喔，凱撒！

安東尼：你的心仁慈善良，儘管哭吧。我發現悲傷是會傳染的——因我看到你流出的哀傷淚珠，我的眼眶亦開始濕潤了。你的主人何在？

僕人：他的營地就在距離羅馬二十哩遠之處。

安東尼：去將所發生之事告訴他。他來此地太危險了，回去將事情告訴他——但是你暫且留下，幫我將遺體抬往市集。我要發表言論，看看人們對這些人所做的染血惡行有何反應。先助我一臂之力，再去將事情的來龍去脈告訴屋大維。

（*安東尼與僕人下，抬著凱撒的遺體。*）

●第二場

（在公共廣場上；布魯圖斯與喀西約上，一群市民隨同而至。）

市民們：要給我們滿意的答覆！

布魯圖斯：那就聽我說吧，朋友們，我會告訴你們凱撒之死的理由。

（布魯圖斯前往講壇。）

市民一：布魯圖斯要說話了，安靜！

布魯圖斯：請耐心聽到最後。各位羅馬人、同胞和朋友們！安靜，聽清楚我說的話，因我的榮譽而相信我，並且尊重我的榮譽，好讓你們相信。用你們的智慧評斷我，喚醒你們的感官知覺，睿智地評斷我。倘若在場有任何人是凱撒的朋友，我要對他說布魯圖斯對凱撒的愛絲毫不亞於他。倘若那位朋友問起布魯圖斯為何起而反抗凱撒，以下是我的答覆：並非我對凱撒的愛減少，而是我對羅馬的愛增加。你們寧可凱撒還活著，而我們至死都淪為奴隸嗎？或者你們寧可凱撒死，而你們卻自由地活著？因凱撒生前愛護我，故我為他而哭泣；因他的幸運，我為他歡喜；因他的英勇，我崇敬他；但是因他的勃勃野心──我殺死了他。在場有誰卑微到甘願為奴？倘若有，請大聲說出來，因為我冒犯了他。在場有誰低劣到不愛自己的國家？倘若有，請大聲說出來，因為我冒犯了他。我暫停發言等待回覆。

全體：沒有，布魯圖斯，沒有這樣的人。

布魯圖斯：那我並未冒犯任何人。（安東尼和其他人上，抬著凱撒的遺體。）他的遺體來了，服喪者是未曾參與謀殺計畫的馬克安東尼，他將也能享有此計畫結果之好處。他和在場的諸位一樣，將在我國的統治階層中有一席之地。我以此作為結語：如同我為了羅馬的福祉而殺死我最好的朋友一般，待我國同胞亦意欲我陪葬之際，我也會用同一把匕首自戕。

全體：活著，布魯圖斯，活著，活下去！

市民一：懷著崇敬護送他回家。

市民二：為他豎立雕像。

市民三：讓他成為凱撒第二。

市民四：讓凱撒的所有榮光歸於布魯圖斯。

布魯圖斯：我的同胞們──

市民二：安靜！靜下來！布魯圖斯要說話了。

布魯圖斯：好同胞們，請容我先行告退。為了我，留在這兒陪伴安東尼，守著尊貴的凱撒的遺體，聆聽我們允許馬克安東尼發表的言論。我懇求各位，莫要離開，除了我以外，直到安東尼語罷方休。

（布魯圖斯下。）

市民一：讓我們聽聽馬克安東尼的說法。

市民三：是啊！讓他站上講壇，我們聽他怎麼說。高貴的安東尼，上去吧！

安東尼：為了布魯圖斯，這是我欠你們的解釋。

（安東尼站上講壇。）

市民四：關於布魯圖斯他有什麼話要說？

市民三：為了布魯圖斯，他欠我們一個解釋。

市民四：他最好莫要在此說布魯圖斯的壞話。

市民一：這個凱撒是一代暴君。

市民三：是啊，此乃無庸置疑，能擺脫他是羅馬的福氣。

安東尼：諸位高尚的羅馬人——

全體：安靜！讓我們聽他說。

安東尼：各位朋友、羅馬人、同胞，請聽我道來！我是來埋葬凱撒，而非讚頌他。但凡人做的惡事，在他們死後將會繼續流傳，善事卻經常隨他們的骨骸而被埋葬。所以，凱撒之事就到此為止吧。尊貴的布魯圖斯告訴你們凱撒野心勃勃；倘若真的如此，那就是重大的疏失了，凱撒已接受嚴厲的懲罰。在此，徵得布魯圖斯和其他人的允許——因布魯圖斯是高尚之人；他們每個人皆是，皆是高尚之人——我前來凱撒的葬禮上發言。他生前是我的好友，對我忠誠而公正，但是布魯圖斯說他野心勃勃，而布魯圖斯亦為高尚之人。凱撒將許多俘虜帶到了羅馬，他們的贖金充滿了公有的國庫。凱撒此舉看似野心勃勃嗎？當窮人哭號之時，凱撒聞之亦啜泣；野心之人應是鐵石心腸，但是布魯圖斯卻說他野心勃勃，而布魯圖斯乃是高尚之人。你們都親眼看到了，在牧神節的盛宴上，我三度將王冠交予他，卻三次都被他回絕；他這是野心嗎？但是布魯圖斯說他野心勃勃，而他確實是高尚之人。我此言並非駁斥布魯圖斯方才的話，只是將我的所知說出來罷了。你們都曾經愛戴凱撒，這不是毫無原因的，那麼你們如今是因何理由而不為他服喪哀悼？喔，判斷力，你已逃向野蠻殘酷的野獸，人們喪失了他們的理智！（他哭泣。）請聽我說完。我的心已隨凱撒進入棺木，我必須暫停發言，等待它回到我的胸膛。

市民一：我認為他言之有理。

市民二：你聽見他說的話了？凱撒不願接下王冠，由此可知他並無野心。

市民三：凱撒似乎是被冤枉了。

市民四：若真如此，有人必須為此付出代價！

市民二：可憐的安東尼！你們看——他哭紅的眼睛有如火焰一般。

市民三：在羅馬沒有比安東尼更高尚的人了。

市民四：你們聽，他又開口說話了。

安東尼：就在昨日，凱撒一言可抵全世界，如今他卻躺在這兒，怎麼沒個像樣的尊重？喔，諸位主人啊！倘若我意圖挑起你們的憤怒，那我就是待布魯圖斯和喀西約不公，你們都知道他們皆為高貴之人，我是不會冤枉他們的。我寧可待死者不公，待我自己和你們不公，也不願冤枉如此高尚之人。但是這裡有張凱撒封緘的字條，是我在他的櫥櫃中找到的；此乃他的遺囑。倘若平凡百姓聽了內容，他們會衝上前去親吻凱撒遺體上的傷口，用他們的手帕沾浸他的鮮血——是的，乞求他的一根頭髮以示追憶，臨死前會在他們遺囑中提及，當作傳家之寶似地傳承給他們的子孫。

市民四：宣讀遺囑吧，馬克安東尼！

全體：遺囑！讓我們聽聽凱撒的遺囑。

安東尼：有點耐心，朋友們，我不能宣讀內容。你們並非草木，亦非石頭，而是活生生的人，聽了凱撒的遺囑必會勃然大怒，內容會使你們氣憤難平。你們最好不要知道你們是他的繼承人，因你們若是知道了，結果會是如何？

市民四：宣讀遺囑，我們會洗耳恭聽，安東尼。

安東尼：告知你們此事已是我踰越之舉，恐怕我會冤枉用匕首刺死凱撒的那些高尚之人。

市民四：他們都是叛徒，而非高尚之人！

全體：遺囑！宣讀遺囑！

市民二：他們是惡徒、殺人兇手！遺囑！宣讀遺囑！

安東尼：難道你們要逼迫我宣讀內容？在凱撒的遺體四周圍成一圈，仔細看著寫下遺囑的他。要我步下講壇嗎？我是否徵得你們的允許？

全體：下來吧！

（*安東尼步下講壇。*）

市民三：圍成一圈，聚集在一起。

市民四：從遺體旁邊退開。

市民二：騰出空間給高尚的安東尼。

安東尼：倘若你們有淚，就準備淚灑當場吧。你們都認得這件斗篷。我猶記得凱撒初次穿上它，是在一個夏日的傍晚，在他的營帳內；那天，他打了一場大勝仗。你們看，喀西約的匕首刺進了這裡，看看妒忌的喀司加造成的傷口，而他最好的朋友布魯圖斯則是刺進這裡。在他拔出他那被詛咒的刀刃之際，看看凱撒的鮮血如何隨之飛濺，彷彿急欲衝出來確定如此殘忍刺殺之人是否真為布魯圖斯，因你們都知道布魯圖斯曾是凱撒的天使。喔，眾神啊，凱撒是那麼地愛他！這是最冷酷無情的一刀，因高尚的凱撒在看他刺殺之時，他偉大的內心亦有如刀割。偉大的凱撒倒下了。喔，他是徹底地被擊垮了，我的同胞們！然後我和你們，在染血的叛逆事件發生在我們身邊之際，我們所有的人都隨之倒地。喔，此刻你們哭泣了，我知道你們感受到憐憫的力量。這些眼淚都是慈悲的。善良的靈魂們，你們只看到凱撒被劃破的斗篷，何以啜泣如此？看看這兒。(他掀開凱撒的斗篷。)這才是他本人──你們看，他被叛徒們刺死了。

市民一：喔，悲慘的景象！

市民二：喔，高尚的凱撒！

市民三：喔，令人悲痛的一天！

市民四：喔，最血腥的景象！

市民一：我們誓必復仇。

全體：復仇！讓我們去找他們！燒吧！殺啊！叛徒們不留活口！

安東尼：且慢，各位同胞。

市民一：安靜，聽好！聽聽高尚的安東尼怎麼說。

市民二：我們聽他說，我們要追隨他，我們要與他同生共死！

安東尼：諸位好友，切莫讓我激怒你們。參與此舉者皆為高尚之人，我不知道他們為何這麼做，因他們既睿智又高尚，他們必定會給你們合理的原因。我並非來此掠奪你們的心志，畢竟我不似布魯圖斯那般能言善道；各位都知道，我是個深愛好友的率直、駑鈍之人，我只是用未假修飾的詞語把你們已經知道的事告訴你們。我必須請求這些傷口，這些可憐而不能言的嘴，代替我來發言。但倘若我是布魯圖斯，而布魯圖斯是安東尼，那麼就會有個安東尼來激奮你們的精神，直到凱撒身上的每個傷口都大聲呼喊，撼動羅馬的基石使之起而暴動。

全體：我們要復仇！

市民一：我們要燒毀布魯圖斯的住所！

市民三：走吧，揪出那些密謀之人！

安東尼：請聽我一言，同胞們，你們都忘了我方才提及的遺囑。

全體：遺囑！讓我們留下來聽聽遺囑的內容吧。

安東尼：此乃凱撒封緘之遺囑，它給予每位羅馬市民七十五枚德拉克馬銀幣。

市民二：高尚的凱撒！我們要為你復仇！

安東尼：他還將他於台伯河畔所有的步道、他的私人涼亭、新種植的蘭花和台伯河，悉數留給你們，留給你們和你們的子子孫孫永世同享。這兒曾有一位凱撒！幾時才會再有像他這般的人？

市民一：再也不會有了！走吧，我們走！我們將他的遺體抬往聖殿火化，再用燃燒的火棍點燃叛徒們的住所。把遺體抬起來！

市民二：去拿火把。

市民三：拆毀他們的住所、椅凳、窗——悉數拆盡！

（市民們抬著遺體下。）

安東尼：現在就行動吧。麻煩，你獲釋了，想去哪兒便去吧。（一名僕人上。）你有何事，朋友？

僕人：閣下，屋大維已來到羅馬，他和雷比達正在凱撒的家中。

安東尼：我會直接過去。

僕人：他說布魯圖斯和喀西約像發了狂似地逃離羅馬。

安東尼：他們可能是聽到我方才撼動人心的那番話。帶我去找屋大維。

（他們下。）

第四幕

● 第一場 ——————————————————P. 083

（在羅馬的一棟房子。安東尼、屋大維與雷比達圍著一張桌子同坐。）

安東尼：這些密謀者都得死，他們的姓名已經註記。

屋大維：你的兄弟也必須死，你同意嗎，雷比達？

雷比達：我同意，唯有一個條件——令姐之子普布利烏斯也得死。

安東尼：同意。你看，我亦註記了他的姓名。好了，雷比達，去凱撒的家中，取得遺囑，好讓我們想想該如何減少他留給人民的遺產金額。

（雷比達下。）

安東尼：走了一個不重要的人，很適合派他去跑腿。真的要讓他與我們平分權力嗎？

屋大維：當你在聽從他的建議決定誰生誰死之時，你是這麼想的。

安東尼：屋大維，我比你多長了幾年的見識。我們加諸榮譽在此人身上，是為了減少我們些許的罪責，他會如同驢子馱著黃金似地背負這些榮耀，在荷重的同時呻吟和大汗淋漓；我們在指引前路，他若非受人引領就是被驅遣。待他將我們的寶藏運送到目的地，我們就卸下他的貨物，把他當隻驢子似地打發他走，讓他抖抖耳朵去草地上覓食。

屋大維：你想怎麼做都隨便你，但他是個名副其實的英勇士兵。

安東尼：我的馬匹亦然，屋大維——我給牠乾草以示獎賞，牠是一隻畜牲，我教牠打鬥、轉彎、停止、前進，牠的身體是由我的心志在控制的。就某些方面而言，雷比達亦是如此；只把他當成財產即可。現在，聽聽我帶來的這個消息：布魯圖斯和喀西約正在召募軍隊，我們必須立即行動，就讓我們聚集最可靠的朋友們開會商議吧，我們必須決定因應的對策。

（他們下。）

● 第二場 ——————————————————— P. 085

（在希臘的一處軍營；鼓聲響起；布魯圖斯、盧西留斯、盧修斯與士兵們上，提第尼烏斯與平達路斯前來與他們會合。）

布魯圖斯：盧西留斯，喀西約是否就在附近？

盧西留斯：是的，平達路斯已帶來他的主人喀西約的問候。

布魯圖斯：我接受他的問候。喀西約如何接待你？告訴我。

盧西留斯：禮貌周到又敬意十足——但是沒有過去待我那般的友善了。

布魯圖斯：你形容的是一個熱情轉淡的朋友。當愛開始生厭和衰退之時，就會變成被強迫的儀式了。坦率而樸真的信仰是沒有詭詐手段的，但是虛偽之人可比賽前的馬匹，看似精神抖擻又表現得很英勇，實則在比賽時垂頭喪氣，因虛假和筋疲力竭而輸了比賽。他的軍隊來了嗎？

盧西留斯：他們有意今晚在這附近紮營，有些人已經跟著喀西約來到此地。

（喀西約與他的士兵們上。）

布魯圖斯：你們聽，他來了。

喀西約（對布魯圖斯）：你置我於不義。

布魯圖斯：眾神啊！我會陷我的敵人們於不義嗎？倘若不會，我又如何會陷自己兄弟於不義？

喀西約：你用演技藏起了過錯，當你這麼做時——

布魯圖斯：喀西約，安靜！我們就別在雙方的軍隊眼前爭執了，應該只讓他們看到我們心中的愛。叫他們退下吧，然後你再去我的營帳中訴說你的怨憤，我會洗耳恭聽。

喀西約：平達路斯，命令我們的軍官們帶領他們的士兵們稍稍退離此地。

布魯圖斯：盧西留斯，你也一樣，莫讓任何人前來我們的營帳，直到我們開會商議完為止。盧修斯和提第尼烏斯來守門吧。

（全體下。）

（布魯圖斯的營帳；布魯圖斯與喀西約上，兩人爭吵。）

喀西約：此乃你陷我於不義之處：你公開指控盧修斯佩拉收賄，因我與他熟識，故我寫了一封信為他辯解，然而你卻忽視我所言。

布魯圖斯：你寫那封信就陷自己於不義。

喀西約：在此般的處境中，批評每個小疏失是不智之舉。

布魯圖斯：讓我來告訴你吧，喀西約，你自己就經常被指為貪財。有人說你為了黃金，不惜將榮譽賣給不應得之人。

喀西約：我──貪財？倘若你不是布魯圖斯，我對眾神發誓，你這番話將成為你的遺言。

布魯圖斯：倘若你不是喀西約，你早已受到懲罰。

喀西約：懲罰？

布魯圖斯：還記得三月十五日嗎？偉大的朱利厄斯不是因公平正義而淌血嗎？哪個惡徒不是以公平正義為理由刺死了他？難道我們如今要被賄賂沾污手指和出賣自己的名譽？我寧可化成一條狗對著月亮狂吠，也不想再當此般的羅馬人了。

喀西約：布魯圖斯，莫要抨擊我！我不會默默隱忍的。我是一名軍人，經驗豐富老練，比你更有決策的能力。

布魯圖斯：不，你不是，喀西約。

喀西約：我是。

布魯圖斯：我說你不是。

喀西約：夠了！顧及你的身體健康，莫要挑唆我，否則我會情緒失控。

布魯圖斯：你走吧，微不足道的人！

喀西約：你説什麼？

布魯圖斯：聽我説，因我有話要説。難道要我容忍你的暴躁脾氣嗎？

喀西約：喔，眾神啊！非得要我受到如是的對待嗎？

布魯圖斯：不僅如此，還有更多，恐怕會直到你驕傲的心崩潰為止。去讓你的奴隸們看看你有多激動，讓他們全身顫抖。要我屈服於你的憤怒情緒嗎？但請眾神見證，你會消化你憤怒的毒藥，甚至讓你撕心裂肺。從今日起，我只會嘲笑你暴躁的脾氣。

喀西約：難道事已至此？

布魯圖斯：你説你是比我更好的軍人，證明給我看，讓我也能心服口服。我向來樂於師法高尚之人。

喀西約：你在各方面都冤枉我了，布魯圖斯，我是説更老練的軍人，而非更好。我有説「更好」嗎？

布魯圖斯：即便你有説，我也不在乎。

喀西約：即使凱撒也從不敢如此激怒我！

布魯圖斯：夠了！是你不敢挑唆他。

喀西約：莫要濫用我的愛，我可能會做出讓自己也後悔的事。

布魯圖斯：你已經做了。你的威脅嚇唬不了我，喀西約，因我有高尚的名譽可防身，威脅只似風一般吹過我身旁。我派遣一名信差去向你索討黃金，而你卻拒我於門外。我不會用不正當的手段取得金錢；我寧可從我的心臟和鮮血中搾取金錢，也不願壓榨農民的辛苦錢。你不願協助我支餉給我的軍隊，也要我以其人之道還治其人之身嗎？當馬可斯布魯圖斯變得貪婪無度，甚至背著他的朋友們藏起如此的垃圾之時，請眾神備齊所有的雷電將他劈成碎片！

喀西約：我並未拒你於門外。愚蠢的信差帶回了錯誤的答覆，致使布魯圖斯傷透了我的心。朋友應該接受朋友的疏失，然而你卻放大檢視我的疏失。

布魯圖斯：我並未如此，直到你如是對待我。

喀西約：你對我毫無感情。

布魯圖斯：我確實不喜歡你的疏失。

喀西約：身為朋友不應在乎如此的疏失。

布魯圖斯：阿諛奉承之人才會如此──即便疏失大如高山。

喀西約：來吧，安東尼，還有年輕的屋大維！只針對喀西約一人復仇吧，因喀西約已經厭世！被他視同手足之人所憎惡，當成奴隸一般地斥責，羅列他所有的疏失當著他的面──數落。喔，我不如哭瞎這雙眼睛吧！這是我的匕首，（*他將他的匕首交給布魯圖斯。*）這是我袒露的胸口，我的心臟就在其內，倘若你是個羅馬人，就將它剜出來吧。我曾拒絕給你黃金，所以我付出我的心臟作為補償。如同你對付凱撒那般地刺死我，我知道當你最是憎惡他之時，你仍然愛他更甚於你愛喀西約。

布魯圖斯：收起你的匕首吧，此事莫再提起。你心中的憤怒有如打火石──只消用力一擊，就會迅速擦出火花，之後須臾即重回原本的冰冷。

喀西約：難道喀西約活著，只是在他的暴躁脾氣激怒布魯圖斯之時成為他的笑柄嗎？

布魯圖斯：當我說出此言之時，我亦是脾氣暴躁。

喀西約：你承認了？把你的手給我。

布魯圖斯：我的心也給你。

（*他們握手。*）

喀西約：喔，布魯圖斯！

布魯圖斯：怎麼了？

喀西約：當我母親生給我的暴躁脾氣使我失態之時，你對我的愛不夠原諒我的過失嗎？

布魯圖斯：我可以做到，喀西約。從今爾後，當你再對布魯圖斯發脾氣時，他會想著是你母親在斥責他，不再怪罪於你。

詩人（從舞台後方）：讓我去見見他們。他們兩人起了口角衝突，此刻不宜讓他們單獨相處。

盧西留斯（從舞台後方）：你不能進去。

第四幕

第三場

詩人（從舞台後方）：唯有死亡才能阻止我。

（一名詩人上，盧西留斯、提第尼烏斯與盧修斯尾隨在後。）

喀西約：發生了什麼事？怎麼了？

詩人：真是可恥，兩位將軍！這是怎麼回事？友愛如常，這才是你們應該做的。仔細聽，因我比你們虛長了幾歲。

喀西約：哈哈！這位詩人竟然不懂得押韻！

布魯圖斯：滾出去吧，你這放肆的傢伙！滾！

（詩人下。）

布魯圖斯：盧西留斯和提第尼烏斯，下令讓軍官們帶著他們的部屬就寢吧。

喀西約：隨後即刻來找我們，帶著梅薩拉一起來。

（盧西留斯與提第尼烏斯下。）

布魯圖斯：盧修斯，來點酒！

（盧修斯下。）

喀西約：我想不到你會如此暴怒。

布魯圖斯：喔，喀西約，我是因為哀傷而心煩意亂。

喀西約：屈服於偶發的惡事不是你一貫的作風。

布魯圖斯：沒人承受得了此般的傷痛。我必須告訴你，波西亞死了。

喀西約：什麼？波西亞？

布魯圖斯：她死了。

喀西約：我方才使得你如此惱怒，何以能逃過被殺害的命運？喔，如此的喪妻之痛！她是死於何病症？

布魯圖斯：她是死於思念我——憂愁於屋大維和馬克安東尼的日益茁壯。我聽聞她在臨死前陷入了憂鬱狀態，待她的僕人們離開之後，她吞下了燃燒中的火炭。

喀西約：她是這樣死的？

布魯圖斯：是的。

喀西約：喔，不朽的眾神啊！

（盧修斯再上，帶著酒和一支蠟燭。）

布魯圖斯：莫再提起她。給我酒，我要一醉解千愁，喀西約。（他飲酒。）

喀西約：我心渴望那高尚的敬酒！斟滿吧，盧修斯，直到酒溢出杯緣為止。布魯圖斯的愛我再多也飲不夠。（他飲酒。）

（盧修斯下，提第尼烏斯與梅薩拉上。）

布魯圖斯：請進，提第尼烏斯！梅薩拉！讓我們同坐在燭火旁，討論我們該做些什麼。（他們坐下。）梅薩拉，我收到幾封信，得知年輕的屋大維和馬克安東尼帶領千軍萬馬要對付我們，他們朝著腓立比前進。

梅薩拉：我也收到幾封信告知相同的訊息。

布魯圖斯：還有其他的事嗎？

梅薩拉：有的，屋大維、安東尼和雷比達處死了上百名元老院議員，奪取了他們的財產。

布魯圖斯：讓我們開始商討我們這些一息尚存知人所要面對的事吧。你對出兵腓立比有何看法？

喀西約：我認為此乃不智之舉。

布魯圖斯：理由何在？

喀西約：是這樣的：最好讓敵人主動找上我們，讓他們耗盡糧食軍需，讓他們的將士精疲力竭，使他們的軍力耗損，此間我們只消休養生息、提高警覺、作好萬全準備。

布魯圖斯：這是好理由，但是還有更好的動機。由此地至腓立比的居民，是被迫順服我們的，他們因我們掠奪物資而心生怨恨，待敵人行軍當地時必會鼓動他們加入行列。倘若我們行軍至腓立比與之交鋒，有當地居民作為我們的後盾，我們必能阻絕他們的這個優勢。

喀西約：聽我說，好兄弟──

布魯圖斯：請求你的海涵，我此言尚未盡，你也莫忘我們已向朋友們索討大量物資。我軍已是蓄勢待發，也有充分的發兵理由，唯敵軍日益壯大，我們即便兵力再強也必會被削弱。世事有如潮起潮落，在高潮之際乘勝追擊即可功成名就，否則一生將會荒廢在淺灘與不幸中。我們如今便是航行在滿潮的海上，必須及時順水行舟──否則就可能喪失機會。

喀西約：那就如你所願往前進吧，我們行軍至腓立比與之交戰。

布魯圖斯：在我們商議之時夜幕已悄然低垂，我們也該就寢了。切莫睡得太深太久，稍事休息即可。還有什麼話要說嗎？

喀西約：沒有了。晚安，我們明日一早便起身啟程。

布魯圖斯：再會了，梅薩拉與提第尼烏斯。高尚的喀西約，晚安，好好休息吧。

喀西約：喔，我親愛的兄弟！今晚有個如此不祥的開始，但願你我之間莫再有如此的歧見，布魯圖斯。

布魯圖斯：目前是安然無事。

喀西約：晚安，閣下。

（全體下，只留下布魯圖斯，他召喚盧修斯，叮嚀他睡在帳內；盧修斯熟睡，布魯圖斯在燭光下看書。）

布魯圖斯：這燭光如此地微弱！（凱撒的鬼魂上。）來者何人？想必是我兩眼昏花才看到這可怕的幻影。它過來了！你是否真的存在？你是神或天使，抑或是魔鬼，使我背脊發涼、汗毛直豎？告訴我你是什麼。

鬼魂：你的邪靈，布魯圖斯。

布魯圖斯：你為何而來？

鬼魂：要讓你知道你將在腓立比見到我。

布魯圖斯：什麼！我會再見到你？

鬼魂：是的，在腓立比。

布魯圖斯：那好吧，我就在腓立比與你再見。（*鬼魂下。*）現在
　　我已鼓起勇氣，你卻消失無蹤！邪靈，我要與你多談幾
　　句。孩子！盧修斯！醒一醒！

（*盧修斯醒來。*）

盧修斯：主人？

布魯圖斯：捎個信給喀西約，請他一大早便領軍啟程，我們隨
　　後就到。

盧修斯：我必達成使命，主人。

（*他們下。*）

第五幕

●第一場

（在腓立比的平原；屋大維、安東尼與他們的軍隊上。）

屋大維：如今我們的願望已然實現。你說敵人不會過來，只
　　會守在山頭和地勢較高之處；結果並非如此，他們的軍隊
　　步步逼近，意欲在腓立比與我們對戰。

安東尼：毋需擔憂，我太瞭解他們了。他們是要我們認為他們
　　很英勇，但其實不然。

（一名信差上。）

信差：請作好準備，兩位將軍，敵人已揮兵前來，必須即刻迎
　　戰。

安東尼：屋大維，你領軍前往戰場的左側。

屋大維：我往右側，你去左側。

安東尼：你何以在此刻與我作對？

屋大維：我並未與你作對，但是我日後就會。

（鼓聲響起；布魯圖斯、喀西約與他們的軍隊上，盧西留斯、提第尼烏
　斯與梅薩拉隨之上。）

布魯圖斯：他們已然止步，意欲與我們商談。

喀西約：堅守陣地，提第尼烏斯。

屋大維：安東尼，我們要不要開戰？

安東尼：不，我們先等他們進攻。往前走，將領們有事相談。

（將領們各自往前走。）

布魯圖斯：君子先禮而後兵，是這樣嗎，同胞們？

屋大維：我們並非樂於守禮之人——如你這般。

布魯圖斯：好言相談勝過兩軍惡鬥，屋大維。

安東尼：是你用惡鬥召來此番好言相談。我指的是你在凱撒

心頭刺穿的那個洞，
呼喊著「萬歲！凱撒
萬福！」

喀西約：你惡鬥的威力
仍是不得而知，但是
你在凱撒葬禮上的
一番談話，無異於當
著蜜蜂的面搶走牠們
的蜂蜜。

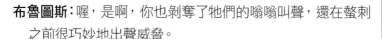

安東尼：但是未拔去牠
們的刺。

布魯圖斯：喔，是啊，你也剝奪了牠們的嗡嗡叫聲，還在螫刺
之前很巧妙地出聲威脅。

安東尼：不像你們這些惡徒連聲也不吭，用匕首刺穿凱撒身
體的兩側，如猩猩一般露出牙齒，像奴隸似地俯首親吻凱
撒的雙腳，而喀司加卻像狗一樣咬住他的脖子！阿諛奉承
之人！

喀西約（*提醒布魯圖斯他有意在三月十五日殺死安東尼*）：這下，布
魯圖斯，這就要怪你自己了。倘若當時依了喀西約的心意
行事，如今這舌頭就不會在此出言不遜了。

屋大維：倘若爭論使我們激動出汗，付諸於行動將化為腥紅
的鮮血。你瞧，我拔劍對付密謀者。（*他拔出了他的劍。*）除
非替凱撒身上的三十三道傷口報了仇，或是我死於叛徒們
的劍下，否則我是不會收劍的！

布魯圖斯：你不會死在叛徒們的手中，除非你帶他們共赴黃
泉！

屋大維：希望如此。我並非生來就注定要死在布魯圖斯的劍下。

布魯圖斯：若你是家族中最高尚之人，那你就不可能有更光榮的死法。

屋大維：安東尼，我們走吧！叛徒們，我們公然挑釁你們，倘若你們今日膽敢迎戰，就前往戰場吧；若非如此，就等你們鼓起勇氣再行接招。

（屋大維、安東尼與他們的軍隊下。）

喀西約：暴風雨已降臨，一切都暴露在危險中。

布魯圖斯：盧西留斯，聽我說，我有話與你相談。

（盧西留斯往前走，他與布魯圖斯退到一旁商談。）

喀西約：梅薩拉！

梅薩拉（往前站）：將軍？

喀西約：梅薩拉，今天是我的生日，喀西約就在這一天誕生。把你的手給我，為我見證我是百般不情願而被迫以我們的自由為賭注，冒險在此役中孤注一擲。你知道我從不相信預兆，但是此刻我已改變心意。渡烏和烏鴉飛越我們的頭頂，低頭看著我們，彷彿我們是病弱的獵物一般；牠們的影子似乎是致命的幡蓋，而我們的軍隊掩護於其下準備赴死。

梅薩拉：切莫相信此等謬論！

喀西約：我並未全盤皆信，因我在精神上已準備好面對所有的危險。（回到布魯圖斯身旁。）現在，高尚的布魯圖斯，既然未來不可確知，那就先作最壞的打算吧。倘若我們此役戰敗，那這就是我們最後一次談話了。所以你決意怎麼做？

布魯圖斯：我始終責怪老加圖的自我了斷，我不知道原因何在，但是我覺得因恐懼可能發生的事而結束自己的生命是懦弱之舉，勇於面對未來才是理所應當。

喀西約：所以倘若我們戰敗，你甘願被戰勝者領著在羅馬街頭遊行示眾？

布魯圖斯：不，喀西約，不！切莫以為布魯圖斯會被人套上枷鎖回到羅馬。在三月十五日起頭之事，就讓我們結束它吧。我不知道我們能否再相見，所以就讓我們再最後一次道別。永別了，喀西約！倘若我們能再相見，那自然是可喜之事；倘若不能，我們就此別過吧。

喀西約：永別了，布魯圖斯！倘若我們能再相見，那就微笑置之；倘若不能，果真就此別過吧。

（全體下。）

●第二場 ──────────────── P. 107

（在戰場上，號角聲響起；布魯圖斯與梅薩拉上。）

布魯圖斯：快馬加鞭，梅薩拉，將這幾道命令送去給戰場彼端的軍隊。（他將字條交給梅薩拉。）（洪亮的號角聲響起。）讓他們即刻發動進攻，因我認為我看出屋大維的軍隊有一弱點。快馬加鞭，梅薩拉！讓他們全軍前來進攻吧。

（全體下。）

●第三場 ——————————— P. 108

（在戰場上的另一區，號角聲響起；喀西約與提第尼烏斯上。）

喀西約：你瞧，提第尼烏斯，看那些惡徒們四下逃竄！我已將敵軍變成我自己的人。這名護旗手本想逃跑，我殺了那個懦夫，搶走了軍旗。

提第尼烏斯：喔，喀西約，布魯圖斯太早放話了。他占了優勢，但是他過於急切，他的士兵們四處劫掠，如今安東尼的手下已包圍我們。

（平達路斯上。）

平達路斯：離開此地，閣下，快逃！馬克安東尼已至你的帳內，閣下。

喀西約：這座山頭已經夠遠了。你瞧，提第尼烏斯，起火燃燒的可是我的營帳？

提第尼烏斯：是的，閣下。

喀西約：提第尼烏斯，快！策馬前去一探究竟，查明那些軍隊是友或敵。

提第尼烏斯：我會如思緒一般儘快趕回來。

（提第尼烏斯下。）

喀西約：平達路斯，登上那座山頭更高處。看好提第尼烏斯，再將你所見向我彙報。（平達路斯爬上山頭。）我在這一天呼吸了第一口氣，如今是風水輪流轉，我將在誕生

之處終結我的一生。我的時日已然無多。（對平達路斯：）告訴我，有何消息？

平達路斯（大喊）：喔，閣下！提第尼烏斯已被騎兵們包圍，他們高聲歡呼，他看似已成俘虜啊！

喀西約：下來，莫要再看。喔，我真是個懦夫，竟活著眼看我最好的朋友在我眼前被人俘虜！（平達路斯從山頭下來。）過來，平達路斯。還記得我在帕提亞俘虜了你嗎？那日，我饒你不死，逼你承諾從此聽從我的吩咐。來吧，信守你的誓言，你如今自由了，用刺進凱撒腹部的這把劍刺穿我的心臟。莫再多言，來，握住劍柄，趁我此刻蒙住了臉，揮劍吧。（平達路斯刺向喀西約。）凱撒，你的血仇已報，甚至用的是殺死你的劍！

（喀西約死去。）

平達路斯：如今我自由了，但是我寧可不用此法重拾我的自由。喔，喀西約！我將逃離此地，遠赴羅馬人尋不著我之處。

（平達路斯下，提第尼烏斯與梅薩拉上。）

梅薩拉：目前為止是兩軍扯平，提第尼烏斯。布魯圖斯對戰屋大維是略勝一籌，但喀西約的軍隊卻慘遭安東尼擊潰。

提第尼烏斯：這消息足以令喀西約欣慰。

梅薩拉：你臨行前他在何處？

提第尼烏斯：在這座山頭上，和他的奴隸平達路斯在一起。

梅薩拉：躺在地上的不就是他嗎？

提第尼烏斯：是的，確實是他，梅薩拉──但是喀西約已然斷氣。喔，落日啊，你今晚西沉時發出滿天紅光，喀西約亦在鮮紅的血泊中駕鶴西歸。羅馬的烈日落下了！我們的時日已無多，他想必是以為我們已經戰敗。

梅薩拉：喔，真是天大的誤會啊！

提第尼烏斯：平達路斯何在？

梅薩拉：快去找他，提第尼烏斯，我去和高貴的布魯圖斯會合，將喀西約的死訊告訴他。

提第尼烏斯：快去，梅薩拉。（*梅薩拉下。*）你何以派我前去，喀西約？我不是去見你的朋友們了嗎？難道你沒聽見他們的歡呼聲？你誤解了一切！但是且慢，將這花冠戴在你的頭上。布魯圖斯要我將它交予你，我這就照辦了。來吧，喀西約的劍，刺向提第尼烏斯的心臟吧。（*他自盡。*）

（*梅薩拉上，帶著布魯圖斯、年輕的加圖與其他人。*）

布魯圖斯：梅薩拉，喀西約的遺體何在？

梅薩拉：就在那兒，提第尼烏斯正在哀悼他。

布魯圖斯：提第尼烏斯面朝上躺臥在地。

加圖：他已死於非命。

布魯圖斯：喔，凱撒，你仍是萬夫莫敵！你的亡靈在世間遊走，讓我們用劍刺向自己的身體。

加圖：英勇的提第尼烏斯！瞧他如何為死去的喀西約加冕！

布魯圖斯：還有如他倆這般的羅馬人仍活在世上嗎？僅存的羅馬人，再會了！羅馬再也不可能有像你們這般的人了。朋友們，我要為此人淌下的淚水尚未流乾。我會再找時間來哀悼你，喀西約，我會再找時間。來吧，朋友們，將他的遺體抬回家安葬。盧西留斯和加圖，讓我們同上戰場吧。現在是三點鐘，羅馬人啊，在夜幕低垂之前我們要發動第二波攻勢碰碰運氣。

（*全體下。*）

●第四場 ————————————— P. 113

（在戰場上的另一區，號角聲響起；士兵們上，打鬥；接著布魯圖斯、年輕的加圖、盧西留斯與其他人上。）

布魯圖斯：各位同胞，抬起你們的頭！

加圖：我們當然會！我要在戰場上高喊我的名字。我是加圖，暴君之敵！

布魯圖斯：我是布魯圖斯，忠於國家之志士！

（布魯圖斯下，年輕的加圖倒地。）

盧西留斯：喔，高尚的加圖，你陣亡了嗎？哎呀，你和提第尼烏斯一樣英勇地死去！

士兵一（對盧西留斯）：不投降就受死吧！

盧西留斯：我寧死也不投降。殺了我吧，你們殺死布魯圖斯，將因他之死而備受崇敬。

士兵二：告訴安東尼，布魯圖斯已成我們的俘虜。

士兵一：將軍來了。（安東尼上。）布魯圖斯被俘！布魯圖斯被俘了，閣下！

安東尼（環顧四周）：他在何處？

盧西留斯：很安全，安東尼，他的安全無虞。我向你保證，敵人決不可能活捉高貴的布魯圖斯。不，眾神將捍衛他，不使他蒙受如此大的屈辱！

安東尼（對士兵一）：這不是布魯圖斯，朋友，但我向你保證他仍是一大戰獲，他只是為了保護布魯圖斯而偽裝，保住此人之性命。請你們善待他，如此之人我寧可與之為友，而非為敵。去吧，看看布魯圖斯是生或死，再到屋大維的營帳知會我們。

（全體下。）

第五幕

第四場

（在戰場上的另一區。布魯圖斯與史特拉托上。）

布魯圖斯：來吧，朋友，在這岩石上休息。看來我們是不可能
　　　　戰勝了，凱撒的鬼魂昨晚現身在我面前，我知道我的死辰
　　　　將至。

史特拉托：非也，閣下。

布魯圖斯：是的，我確信是如此。你也看到戰況了，我們被
　　　　敵人打得潰不成軍，與其坐以待斃，不如自我了斷。史特
　　　　拉托，你是個備受尊崇之人，你此生已有榮譽加身。拿著
　　　　我的劍吧，轉過頭去，莫要看著我伏劍而死好嗎，史特拉
　　　　托？

史特拉托：先把你的手給我。再會了，閣下。

布魯圖斯：再會了，好史特拉托。（他衝向他的劍。）凱撒，你安
　　　　息吧！我殺死你亦是存著此般的善念啊。

（布魯圖斯死去；號角聲響起；屋大維、安東尼、梅薩拉、盧西留斯與
　軍隊上。）

屋大維：那是什麼人？

梅薩拉：我主子的僕人。史特拉托，你的主人何在？

史特拉托：從束縛你的奴隸身分解脫了，梅薩拉。征服者只能
　　　　一把火燒了他，因唯有布魯圖斯才能征服布魯圖斯，沒有
　　　　別人能因他的死而獲得榮耀。

盧西留斯：本應如此。我要感謝你，布魯圖斯，你證明了盧西
　　　　留斯的所言不假。

屋大維：但凡曾為布魯圖斯效力之人，我皆願為我所用。朋
　　　　友，你願為我效力嗎？

史特拉托：是的，只要有梅薩拉的推薦。

屋大維：推薦他吧，好梅薩拉。

梅薩拉：我的主人是怎麼死的，史特拉托？

史特拉托：我手握著劍，他衝向那把劍自盡。

梅薩拉：屋大維，讓他跟隨你吧，他已最後一次為我的主人效忠。

安東尼（恭敬地）：這是最崇高的羅馬人。除了他之外，所有密謀者皆因妒嫉偉大的凱撒而做了謀逆之事。唯有布魯圖斯，他是自命為了全體羅馬人的福祉而下手。他的一生令人欽佩，他身上的種種特質皆使自然之神可能起身對全世界說：「他是個男子漢！」

屋大維：由於他的美德，就讓我們給他萬分崇敬和風光大葬吧。他的遺骨今晚就暫時放在我的帳內，當他是個軍人一般地光榮待之。下令軍隊休息，我們這就離開，共享這可喜之日的榮耀。

（全體下。）

Literary Glossary ● 文學詞彙表

aside 竊語

一種台詞。演員在台上講此台詞時，其他角色是聽不見的。角色通常藉由竊語來向觀眾抒發內心感受。

- Although she appeared to be calm, the heroine's **aside** revealed her inner terror.
  雖然女主角看似冷靜，但她的**竊語**透露出她內在的恐懼。

....

backstage 後台

一個戲院空間。演員都在此處準備上台，舞台布景也存放此處。

- Before entering, the villain impatiently waited **backstage**.
  在上台前，壞人在**後台**焦躁地等待。

....

cast 演員；卡司陣容

戲劇的全體演出人員。

- The entire **cast** must attend tonight's dress rehearsal.
  全體演員必須參加今晚的正式排練。

....

character 角色

故事或戲劇中虛構的人物。

- Mighty Mouse is one of my favorite cartoon **characters**.
  太空飛鼠是我最愛的卡通**人物**之一。

....

climax 劇情高峰

戲劇或小說中主要衝突的結局。

- The outlaw's capture made an exciting **climax** to the story.
  逃犯落網成為故事中最刺激的**精彩情節**。

....

comedy 喜劇

有趣好笑的戲劇、電影和電視劇，並有快樂完美的結局。

■ My friends and I always enjoy a Jim Carrey **comedy**.
我朋友和我總是很喜歡金凱瑞演的**喜劇**。

---

conflict 戲劇衝突

故事主要的角色較量、勢力對抗或想法衝突。

■ *Dr. Jekyll and Mr. Hyde* illustrates the **conflict** between good and evil.
《變身怪醫》描述善惡之間的**衝突**。

---

conclusion 尾聲；結局

解決情節衝突的方法，使故事結束。

■ That play's **conclusion** was very satisfying. Every conflict was resolved. 該劇的**結局**十分令人滿意，所有的衝突都被圓滿解決。

---

dialogue 對白

小說或戲劇角色所說的話語。

■ Amusing **dialogue** is an important element of most comedies.
有趣的**對白**是大多喜劇中重要的元素之一。

---

drama 戲劇

故事，通常非喜劇類型，特別是寫來讓演員在戲劇或電影中演出。

■ The TV **drama** about spies was very suspenseful.
那齣關於間諜的電視**劇**非常懸疑。

---

event 事件

發生的事情；特別的事。

■ The most exciting **event** in the story was the surprise ending.
故事中最精彩的**事件**是意外的結局。

---

introduction 簡介

一篇簡短的文章，呈現並解釋小說或戲劇的劇情。

- The **introduction** to *Frankenstein* is in the form of a letter.
  《科學怪人》的**簡介**是以信件的形式呈現。

motive 動機

一股內在或外在的力量，迫使角色做出某些事情。

- What was that character's **motive** for telling a lie?
  那個角色說謊的**動機**為何？

passage 段落

書寫作品的部分內容，範圍短至一行，長至幾段。

- His favorite **passage** from the book described the author's childhood.
  他在書中最喜歡的**段落**描述了該作者的童年。

playwright 劇作家

戲劇的作者。

- William Shakespeare is the world's most famous **playwright**.
  威廉莎士比亞是世界上最知名的**劇作家**。

plot 情節

故事或戲劇中一連串的因果事件，導致最終結局。

- The **plot** of that mystery story is filled with action.
  該推理故事的**情節**充滿打鬥。

point of view 觀點

由角色的心理層面來看待故事發展的狀況。

- The father's **point of view** about elopement was quite different from the daughter's. 父親對於私奔的**看法**與女兒迥然不同。

prologue 序幕

在戲劇第一幕開始前的介紹。

- The **playwright** described the main characters in the **prologue** to the play.
  劇作家在**序幕**中描述了主要角色。

....

quotation 名句

被引述的文句；某角色所說的詞語；在引號內的文字。

- A popular **quotation** from *Julius Caesar* begins, "Friends, Romans, countrymen . . ."
  《凱撒大帝》中**常被引用的文句**開頭是：「各位朋友，各位羅馬人，各位同胞⋯⋯」。

....

role 角色

演員在劇中揣摩表演的人物。

- Who would you like to see play the **role** of Romeo?
  你想看誰飾演羅密歐這個**角色**呢？

....

sequence 順序

故事或事件發生的時序。

- Sometimes actors rehearse their scenes out of **sequence**.
  演員有時會不按**順序**排練他們出場的戲。

....

setting 情節背景

故事發生的地點與時間。

- This play's **setting** is New York in the 1940s.
  戲劇的**背景設定**於 1940 年代的紐約。

....

soliloquy 獨白

角色向觀眾發表想法的一番言論，猶如自言自語。

- One famous **soliloquy** is Hamlet' speech that begins, "To be, or not to be . . . "
  哈姆雷特最知名的**獨白**是：「生，抑或是死……」。

---

symbol 象徵

用以代表其他事物的人或物。

- In Hawthorne's famous novel, the scarlet letter is a **symbol** for adultery.
  在霍桑知名的小說中，紅字是姦淫罪的**象徵**。

---

theme 主題

戲劇或小說的主要意義；中心思想。

- Ambition and revenge are common **themes** in Shakespeare's plays.
  在莎士比亞的劇作中，野心與報復是常見的**主題**。

---

tragedy 悲劇

嚴肅且有悲傷結局的戲劇。

- *Macbeth*, the shortest of Shakespeare's plays, is a **tragedy**.
  莎士比亞最短的劇作《馬克白》是部**悲劇**。
